"What's going on? That's not social studies."
Marcie was quick to peer over my shoulder.

"I'm practicing Russian in my spare time. See?"
I held up the coded note. Marcie's jaw dropped.
There was no way she could decipher this. I set
to work decoding Spinner's message. Ah. First
word: "Good." I wrote it above Spinner's letters.

"Satch Carlton, if you think I believe you about
practicing Russian, you've got oatmeal between
your ears. You guys are up to something. Let me
see that." She reached for Spinner's note.

I snatched it away just in time and stuffed it in
my mouth.

In a flash Miss Hepburn stood over my desk.
She didn't say a word. She just gave me a cough-
it-up-or-else look. Then she held out her hand.

Ask for these White Horse titles from Chariot Books:

Satch and the New Kid

Just Victoria
More Victoria
Take a Bow, Victoria
Only Kidding, Victoria

SATCH
AND THE
MOTORMOUTH

Karen Sommer

To Larry,
Have some
laughs when
Satch meets the
"Big MM."
Karen Sommer

Chariot Books
DAVID C. COOK PUBLISHING CO.

Dedicated to
Jason and Jeffrey

A White Horse Book
Published by Chariot Books,
an imprint of David C. Cook Publishing Co.
David C. Cook Publishing Co., Elgin, Illinois 60120
David C. Cook Publishing Co., Weston, Ontario

SATCH AND THE MOTORMOUTH
© 1987 by Karen Sommer

Cover illustration by Dennis Hockerman
Design by Rosalie Collins and Barbara Tillman
First Print, 1987
Printed in the United States of America
92 91 90 89 88   2 3 4 5

Library of Congress Cataloging-in-Publication Data
Sommer, Karen,
    Satch and the Motormouth.
    (A White horse book)
    Summary: Sixth-grader Satch, a child of divorced parents,
has to think again about his adversarial relationship with a
girl in his class when he finds out some startling news about
her mother and his father.
    [1. Divorce—Fiction. 2. Schools—Fiction] I. Title.
PZ7.S6963Sat 1987   [Fic]   86-24031
ISBN 1-55513-063-1

Contents

Contents

1
The Motor Arrives

"Flood! Flood! Evacuate the gym," screamed Marcie in feigned panic.

"Knock it off, creep-o," I hollered back. I continued to enter the gym carrying my mammoth-sized science project.

Marcie would have liked nothing better than to turn my masterpiece into one of her natural disasters. She should know. Motormouth Marcie *is* a natural disaster. In the six years I've been forced to be in the same class with that mouth, nothing intelligent has ever come out of it.

"Yuck," she continued to sneer, "I was right. You're going to flood the gym. Either that, or you'll bury us alive in a mud slide. You have nothing there but dirt and water. Honestly, Sidney Carlton, you certainly don't expect a passing grade for a pat-a-cake demonstration, do you?"

"And I suppose your satellite station shows every one of your two IQ points," I snapped back.

"There's no reason to get nasty, *Siiidney,*" Marcie taunted.

"Satch! You know my name is Satch!"

"Such hostility, *Siiidney.* Just because I choose to address you by your proper name. I suppose I should have expected this treatment from an immature sixth grader such as yourself. And all because you are trying to pass off this dilapidated cardboard swamp as a science exhibit. Believe me, Mr. Scientific Zero, Miss Hepburn won't fall for it. You'll flunk for sure. Dirt and water still make mud, no matter how you try to disguise it. And you are still *Siiidney* Carlton, no matter how many times you call yourself Satch."

Motormouth Marcie was shifting into overdrive. Bullets were shooting out like an automatic machine gun. It's beyond me how she could fire words that fast without coming up for air.

"Miss Hepburn isn't dumb, *Siiidney.* She knows a sophisticated science project when she sees one. And she certainly can recognize that your mud pit is lacking for any kind of scientific value." Motormouth Marcie paused long enough to glare in disgust at my project.

The blood inside me was racing around at least two hundred miles an hour. I could feel my face

8

heating up. The vein in my neck was throbbing. Any second, the glowing lump sitting on my shoulders was gonna start whirling around like the red flasher on top of a police car. If I opened my mouth, I'd probably shriek like a siren on a police car.

"I'm really surprised you even bothered to carry in this poor excuse of a project, unless, of course, you were cleaning your filthy locker. And in that case, you will be pleased to know that the trash barrel is right behind you." Marcie pointed and continued with her onslaught of words. "I'm certain that I speak for the entire student body. We would be most grateful if you would deposit your fungus-coated container over there. Undoubtedly, you have contaminated everyone here. The school nurse is contacting the health department at this very moment. Surely, they will have to quarantine the whole school." She drew in one last breath. "And all because of you, *Siiidney* Carlton."

Trying to talk back to Motormouth Marcie was like trying to swim up Niagara Falls. A cold shiver ran down my spine. I mustered what little calm I could find inside myself, and faked a charming retort. "Thank you, Marcie Cook. I deeply appreciate your invaluable critiquing."

Temporarily stunned, Marcie's motor stalled. No one ever agreed with her. It was a brand-new experience. Time to make my escape. I set down my irrigation system at the assigned table and hightailed it across the gym to friendly territory.

"Spinner, wait up," I called.

"Hey, Satch, old buddy," Spinner greeted me with his usual enthusiasm. "Did you find a new motor for your irrigation system?"

"Unfortunately, the only motor over there is the one permanently attached to Marcie's mouth."

Spinner chuckled knowingly. Motormouth Marcie needed no explanation to Spinner. He'd been tied into knots with her tongue a few times himself.

"What you gonna do for an engine?" Spinner questioned.

"I called my dad last night. He's gonna bring one in this morning and help me connect it. Don't worry. He'll be here. Right now, my biggest problem is escaping that mouth. My ears are still ringing."

Spinner snickered, "You think you got it bad. I ran into Lizard-breath Lizabeth this morning. She blows bubbles on her braces. Worse yet, do you know what it's like looking at teeth wearing Tuesday's pizza?"

"Well, at least Lizabeth stops talking long enough to eat."

"You have a point there," laughed Spinner.

Kids and parents were still jamming the entryway of the gym.

"Hey, I think I saw your dad," Spinner announced.

"Great!"

The two of us bolted across the floor. Dad raised his hand in recognition and headed toward Spinner and me. I was glad to see he made it.

"Hi, fellas," Dad greeted us. He opened the bundle he was carrying. "Your project looks pretty sharp, Satch. Too bad the first motor went out on you. This one should do the trick, though."

"Super. Thanks, Dad."

Dad went about connecting the replacement. I inspected the wires. Lookin' good. We turned on the power. Success. The pump sent the water into the reservoir. The dam released the water into the aqueducts. Sprinklerlike holes dispersed the water to the soil. And wha-la, arid desert land became productive farmland. I set a giant poster behind my project to explain the entire process. In real life, rainwater and mountain streams feed the reservoir, but I couldn't wait for the water to evaporate and become a cloud. That's why I needed the pump to retrieve the water and send it back to the reservoir. It was a perfect demonstration, even if Motormouth Marcie didn't think so. What did she know, anyway!

"Hello, Mr. Carlton. Is everything OK?" Marcie politely asked my dad. I should have known Marcie would try to interfere. She sure had Dad fooled. He actually thought of her as human. Marcie continued badgering Dad with questions. "Is there anything I can do to help?"

Hmm . . . since you asked, you could go stick your head inside that volcano over there.

"Oh, hi, Marcie," Dad greeted her extra politely. "Thanks, we're just fine. Putting the finishing

11

touches on Satch's irrigation system."

Ugh! . . . Rescue me from her mission of mercy.

"How's your mom like her new job, Marcie?"
Dad asked.

*Ah, Dad, how could you ask her a question?
She'll get her motor going and we'll be here for
weeks.*

"Mom loves it. She says everyone is really great.
And she loves the computer. Those courses at the
community college were just the thing to bring her
job skills up to date."

Yuck! Put a muffler on it, Marcie.

"Well, we really enjoy seeing a new face down at
the office," Dad added. "Nice to run into you,
Marcie."

Frankly, it would have been a lot nicer to run
into Marcie with a Mack truck.

"Satch, I think you're all set here. I've got to
dash back to the office." Dad patted my shoulder.

"You saved the day, Dad. Thanks."

"See you tonight. Seven o'clock?"

"Yep. Seven o'clock. 'Bye." I waved.

Dad hurried out the door, stopping a second to
greet Miss Hepburn politely. Now she was worth
talking to. Miss Hepburn was plenty sharp. She
was just about the neatest teacher I'd ever had.
School has never been hard or anything for me, but
it's been the big B—boring. Miss Hepburn made
school fun. She knew how to act out the lives of
famous people. She knew how to explain decimals
without kids collapsing in frustration. She even

12

knew how to jazz up dull spelling rules. But the best thing about Miss Hepburn was that she had figured out, right from the start, that I was a genius.

2
Winner Takes All

"Satch," Mom called, "Spinner's family is here to pick you up."

"Coming," I answered, running down the stairs with my tennis shoes in hand.

"Good luck tonight," Mom encouraged.

"Sure you don't want to come?"

"Well, I think it'll be better if I wait at home. You can tell me all about it when you get back. OK?"

"OK."

I tried not to sound disappointed, but I was. Ever since Mom and Dad got divorced, they hated to run into each other at school or church or even at the grocery store. Mom knew Dad would be at

14

school because he helped me with the project. My activities either belonged to Mom *or* Dad, but never to Mom *and* Dad.

Mr. Spinnelli honked again, just as I opened the door and ran out. The Spinnellis were a together family. Spinner never had to worry about his mom running into his dad at a parent-teacher conference. He always knew where he'd spend a holiday. And he didn't have to be careful about mentioning one parent's name in front of the other. The only real problem Spinner had was his four-year-old brother, Frankie. The best way to describe Frankie is to picture a tornado with feet.

I slid onto the seat next to Spinner.

"Hi, Satch," the Spinnellis greeted me.

"Hi. Thanks for the lift."

Frankie started manuevering into position. He crawled over Spinner to lunge toward me with his hand pointing to his mouth. "See? See, Satch?"

"Uh-huh," I answered. What was there to see. The tornado had teeth, a tongue, and pepperoni breath.

"See? It wiggles. See?" He lunged closer and sent more pepperoni my way.

"He's got a loose tooth," Spinner said dryly, rolling his eyes.

Gotch ya, pal. I share your enthusiasm. I rolled my eyes to Spinner in return.

"I'm going to be rich. The tooth fairy likes good teeth. See? No boo-boos." Frankie demonstrated his wiggle several more times.

"Keep brushing, Frank-o." I went along with the gag. *And use some mouthwash while you're at it.*

"Frankie," Spinner interrupted, "why don't you let me try to pull it out for you?"

"NO! NO!" Frankie wailed. "Pinner—don't take my tooth. My money. My tooth. My money."

Man, that kid acts like he has Fort Knox in his mouth.

"Anthony Spinnelli, I told you to leave Frankie alone." Spinner's mother turned around. "That tooth will come out when it's good and ready. And in the meantime, you keep your hands off him."

Spinner rolled his eyes again. Frankie gloated at his apparent victory.

Mr. Spinnelli parked the car, and we filed into the gym for the PTA meeting. The boring stuff would come first: carnival committee report, playground committee report, assembly committee report. The people who ran this event were no fools. They knew announcing the winners of the Science Fair at the end was the only way to make people sit through all their yackety-yak.

"See your dad yet, Satch?" Spinner asked.

"Nope. But he'll be here."

Almost seven o'clock. More and more people were crowding in the doorway. And with them came Motormouth Marcie. As usual, she came charging toward me.

"Well, *Siiidney,* what have you brought this time to churn your dirt and water?"

Marcie wasn't waiting for an answer. She had one

16

all ready to supply. "An eggbeater? Maybe your mommy has some pretty cookie cutters and she'll let you play muddy cakes, if you're extra good."

"Bug off, Marcie, before I put *you* into orbit with your satellite."

"Aha. Resorting to threats now, are we? Not very becoming. Remember, there are witnesses. You can be arrested." Marcie always had to have the last word.

Someday, I'll take that mouth and sew it shut when she's asleep.

"Satch," Dad came puffing in. "Just got here in time. The parking lot out there is jammed."

Dad caught his breath. "Oh, hi, Marcie. Nice to see you again. Just saw your mother looking for a parking space, too."

Hmm. Maybe Marcie's mother will get lucky and won't find one. Then she and Marcie will have to leave.

"Nice to see you, too, Mr. Carlton. I came in to save us seats. We knew it would be crowded."

"Good idea, Marcie. We'd better find a place ourselves," Dad continued.

At last, escape from that motorized gorilla. Any minute she would start beating on her chest.

Dad and I wove our way through the packed gym and sat down behind the Spinnellis.

Dad tapped Mr. Spinnelli on the shoulder. "Thanks for giving Satch a ride."

"Sure thing, Sid," Mr. Spinnelli nodded.

"See? See? My tooth." Frankie Spinnelli was

17

wiggling his tooth right under Dad's nose.

"Oh, yes. My, Frankie, you're certainly growing up fast." Dad played along enthusiastically.

Frankie beamed. The importance of his loose tooth had created instant stardom. Nothing pleased Frankie more than being the center of attention. He wiggled his tooth in front of the Ling family, all nine of them.

"See? Tooth?" Frankie announced.

Mr. Ling smiled and bowed.

"See? Tooth?"

Mrs. Ling smiled and bowed.

"See? Tooth?"

Grandma Ling smiled and bowed.

Frankie was making their Oriental custom look like The Wave in the cheering section of Tiger Stadium. Bow. Bow. Bow. Bow. The Lings had come to America at the end of last summer. They were boat people who had escaped from Vietnam. My church and Spinner's church had sponsored them. That's kinda like adopting the family to get them adjusted to a new life in Owosso.

Now that Frankie had bothered all the people he knew, he started lunging at every stranger he could find to do this tooth-wiggling-pepperoni-breath act.

The PTA meeting finally started. The committee-this and committee-that reports were in progress. Mrs. Spinnelli grabbed Frankie. She sat him in a chair next to her. Soon Frankie was trying to stand up on the chair. If he didn't fall over backwards first, he would undoubtedly turn into a folded-chair

18

sandwich. His mother caught him just in time. She tried to put him on her lap. She must have been crazy to think she could keep a tornado from moving. He twisted down the side of her leg and started crawling along the floor. Frankie was on his way to wiggle his tooth to a fresh supply of people.

"See? See?" I could almost hear his tooth grinding from side to side.

Mrs. Spinnelli whispered something to Mr. Spinnelli. He just shrugged his shoulders. Evidently, Mr. Spinnelli thought Frankie was safer crawling around on the floor wiggling his tooth at people than trying to confine him to a collapsible chair.

The reports were finally over. The PTA president called for attention. "And finally, we would like to award the ribbons to the winners of our Science Fair."

I sat up straight and adjusted my seat. At last, we were getting somewhere.

"As you no doubt have observed," she continued, "we have a fine display of outstanding talent here at Roosevelt School. Each of the thirty projects entered reflects a high standard of achievement. We congratulate you all for a job well done." She was certainly going to prolong this moment as long as possible. "The projects were entered in one of the three categories: independent scientific research, demonstration of a scientific principle, and illustration of science at work in our culture."

I had decided to enter the last category. Since the title was so scary, fewer kids chose it. Actually, it was the easiest category, but I was the only one who figured that out.

I could still hear Frankie Spinnelli in the background, "See? See? No boo-boos in my tooth."

I think Frankie must have been conducting his own science experiment: Just how many wiggles can a baby tooth take before it finally falls out?

"The blue ribbon for scientific research is awarded to Lizabeth Dirkson for her Comparative Analysis of Identical Twins." Lizabeth marched up to the stage. In spite of her lizard breath, Lizabeth had done a fantastic job. She had fingerprinted, photographed, and even cut samples of hair from about twenty sets of twins. Applause greeted Lizabeth. She flashed her braces at the audience, thanked the judges, and stepped down.

The prize for the second category, demonstration of a scientific principle, was about to be awarded. Hai Ling was sure to win. Reading and spelling were sort of tough for Hai, since he had only started learning English six months ago. But Hai was unbeatable at math, science, and art. His display of optical illusions was superb. No one else could even come close.

The speaker on stage continued, ". . . and the winner is Hai Ling." Hai stepped forward, accepted his ribbon, and bowed slightly.

Finally, we were down to the event I'd been waiting away my life for. I held my breath.

". . . and the last blue ribbon belongs to Satch Carlton."

Yeah. I did it. I was a winner.

I scrambled to my feet. Taking two steps at a time, I bounded up onto the stage. I leaned over the microphone, "Thank you very—"

Clunk! Bang! Splat!

"Aaah!" a woman shrieked.

Everyone's head turned.

"Tooth. My tooth. I want my tooth."

"Eeeek! Look out. It's coming our way," shouted another panic-stricken voice.

"MY TOOTH. THE PUDDLE HAS MY TOOTH. I WANT MY MONEY."

Mass confusion was spreading like a chain reaction. Above it all, I could hear Marcie's motor blaring like a foghorn, "IT'S A MUD SLIDE. *SIIIIDNEY* CARLTON, I TOLD YOU THAT WAS NOTHING BUT A MUD SLIDE."

On the floor lay my masterpiece: a collapsed reservoir, disassembled aqueducts, drowned crops, and mud. Mud as far as the eye could see, and it was till oozing in all directions. It covered everything. Floor. Chairs. Even people. An endless ooze. There in the middle, in the eye of the storm, sat Frankie Spinnelli. Dripping with mud from head to toe, he sobbed, "My tooth. That lake drowned my tooth. My money's all gone. No more tooth fairy."

And no more science project either. Frankie Spinnelli had seen to that. He was the real winner: best illustration of science at work in our culture. Some easy category.

21

3
Genius at Work

The tooth fairy left fifty cents anyway for Frankie Spinnelli. Even with that, all Frankie did was complain that the tooth fairy was cheap. He was sure his magnificent tooth was worth at least a whole dollar. Personally, I think the tooth fairy was pretty generous, considering she should have slipped a lawsuit under his pillow for damages to my science project.

The next week at school our class was busy preparing for the fast-approaching valentine party. Miss Hepburn divided the jobs into three committees: decorations, food, and entertainment.

Most of the girls volunteered for the decorations and food. That left A.J., Pete, Hai, Spinner, and me in charge of the fun and games. And fun and games it would be; the five of us knew how to see to that. Miss Hepburn must have been worried, though, because she quickly assigned two girls to our committee. They were none other than Lizard-breath Lizabeth and Motormouth Marcie. What luck. Those two would *work* at spoiling fun.

Marcie started right in, "Well, who's in charge here?" She obviously wanted it to be her.

"Spinner's the committee chairman," I cut in.

"Yeah," the other guys cheered. At least the five of us could stick together. We'd still have control over those two power-hungry animals. I wouldn't allow Marcie to do anything except blink her eyes.

"Well, I have a game to suggest. It's called Veiled Valentine." Marcie started right in wanting her own way.

"What now?" I moaned.

"Just give it a chance. You'll see. It can be lots of fun. We all draw names the week before Valentine's Day. You can't tell whose name you drew. All week long you secretly do something special for that person. People have lots of fun trying to figure out who their valentine is. Then at the party, the secrets are unveiled."

"Oh, yuck," I gagged. "I suppose we all have to wear a veil, too. Marcie, you would look kinda cute as the Bride of Frankenstein."

The guys all laughed.

"Don't be stupid, *Siiidney*. This game can be a lot of fun, if you'd just give it a chance."

"Well, forget it, Marcie," I said authoritatively. "Let a genius get to work. I'll come up with something better than Veiled Valentine."

Marcie couldn't get her way this time. We outnumbered her and she knew it. The guys started brainstorming for some *real* fun.

"I know," I shouted. At last, I had the ultimate idea. "The Great Egg Exchange." I raised my eyebrows to explain my true meaning.

The guys understood, "Yeee-aaah." They signaled back to me.

"What is?" Hai asked.

Hai sometimes needed American customs explained to him. It usually was no trouble, but this was one time I really didn't want to say anything more than necessary. If the girls didn't know what The Great Egg Exchange *actually* meant, so much the better.

"Well-er-ah," Spinner tried to help me out, "people get partners and sort of exchange an egg back and forth. They keep stepping farther and farther apart."

"Oh," Hai nodded. His face still registered confusion.

I tried to flash Hai the no-more-questions-right-now look. He was too busy sorting this new information in his mind.

"Egg, it cooked?" Hai asked suspiciously.

"No," I whispered as low as possible. It wasn't low enough.

"*Siiidney*, you wouldn't dare. There'll be

24

smashed eggs everywhere," Marcie wailed out. "You'll get us all expelled. I'm not gonna get blamed for your shenanigans."

"Cool it, Marcie. Keep your voice down."

"I mean it, *Siiidney.* You won't get me to go along with this. Even if you guys do outvote me, I'll do . . . I'll . . ." Marcie was actually searching for words. "Look, Miss Hepburn may allow some pretty strange things in this classroom, of which, I might add, you are the primary example, but she's not crazy. When she finds out what this committee is up to, she'll cancel the whole party." Marcie's motor had recovered from the temporary setback.

The egg game might be a mess, but we couldn't do any real harm outside. However, considering Marcie's talent for poisoning minds, Miss Hepburn might call off the whole party before we even had a chance to explain.

"Look it, Marcie," I tried to reason, "we're gonna play the game outside. It's just a few eggs. You're not afraid of a few eggs, are you?"

"Well-er-ah," Marcie paused. I must have shamed her into it. She looked over at Lizabeth.

"Come on, girls," Spinner coaxed. "You'll have fun, too."

"Well," Marcie hesitated, "Lizabeth and I will go along with you on one little condition."

Oh, oh. Marcie's little conditions were never little.

"Yeah? What?"

"We'll agree to *your* Great Egg Exchange if

you'll agree to *my* Veiled Valentine game. Deal?"

Boxed in again.

"Deal," we grumbled.

How can one simpleminded girl overpower five tough guys?

4
Barb Who?

Thursday the class hung red and white hearts from the ceiling. We taped valentine folders to each desk. And just before dismissal, we drew names for the Veiled Valentine game.

"Whose name did you draw, Spinner?" I asked.

"Hey, you're not supposed to know."

"I won't tell. Come on. You can let me in on it," I pleaded.

"We-ell, OK. I drew Hai. Who'd you get?"

"The worst. You'll never believe it," I moaned.

"Motormouth Marcie?" Spinner looked horrified.

"No, not quite that bad, but it's a girl. Lizabeth Dirkson."

Spinner doubled over with laughter. "Old Lizard-breath Lizabeth. Ha! Ha! Buy her some toothpicks to clean out her braces. That's hysterical." Spinner broke out in laughter again.

"Sure, Spinner. It's hysterical. I can hardly contain myself."

Friday night Dad picked me up. Every other weekend I spend at his place. Carrie and Lisa, my older sisters, don't go much. That's OK with me. It usually means Dad and I have the whole time to ourselves.

"Ready for homemade chili?" Dad was a terrific cook. He started pulling out the supplies.

"You bet. I'm starved."

"What's happening at school these days, Satch?" Dad started chopping onions.

"Oh, it's about the same, I guess," I answered. I stared at the floor thinking about the *girl's* name I had drawn for Marcie's silly Veiled Valentine gimmick.

"Something on your mind?" Dad could always tell when I was down.

"Sort of."

"Anything I can do?"

"Not really. It's just stupid girls."

"Aaah. I see." Dad nodded his head.

"They mess everything up."

Dad continued shaking his head and smiling.

"Dad, do girls still mess everything up when they get older?"

28

"Well, Satch, people still have problems no matter how old they are. I'm not sure you can blame them all on girls, however."

"Well, you can blame most problems on girls and any leftovers can be credited to Frankie Spinnelli."

Dad started opening a can of tomatoes. "What about your teacher? She's female. I thought you were crazy about her."

"She's different, Dad. She's fun. It's the girls my age. They're turkeys, Dad, regular turkeys."

"Well, when I was eleven, I felt that way, too. Except we thought the girls were dogs," Dad chuckled.

"Then you know what I mean?"

"I know what you mean. But I also know you'll change, and those turkeys will change, too."

Dad started cooking the meat.

"Dad, what did you do when you were my age and had to give a present to a creepy girl?"

"I probably did exactly what you're doing."

"Huh?"

"I complained."

We laughed.

"And what did you do after that?"

"Well, Satch, I went out and bought the present and made the best of the situation even though I didn't want to."

"Somehow, I knew that was the answer," I mumbled.

"Look, Satch, I can't tell you what to do, but I know you're grown up enough not to hurt this girl's feelings just because she's not your favorite person in the world."

"But, Dad, she has lizard breath!"

"I know. And she probably has barnacles growing on her earlobes and a ring through her nose."

"Come on, Dad, I'm serious."

"Well, lizard breath or not, the girl has feelings, just the same as you and me."

"OK. OK. I get your drift."

Brrring. The telephone interrupted.

Dad's hands were full.

I picked up the receiver, "Hello?"

"Sid?" A woman's voice was at the other end. "Is that you?" She sounded surprised.

"No, this is—"

"Satch?" she interrupted. "Is that you?"

"Ah, yeah." *Who is this voice?*

"Is your dad there?"

"Ah, yeah. He's right here," I hesitated.

Dad washed his hands and took the phone anxiously. "Oh, hi. Uh, huh . . . yeah . . . yeah. . . . Well, we were just about to dive into some of my famous chili . . . yeah . . . great . . . not exactly. . . . OK, see ya . . . 'bye."

Who was that? Why was a woman calling Dad?

Awkwardly, Dad hung up the phone and started talking, "Satch, will you hand me the chili beans on the counter?"

I walked over and grabbed the beans.

Quickly, Dad started talking again. "Thanks. And now to add the chili beans." He poured them on.

30

"And the secret ingredient, chili powder. That'll give it some real zing. . . ."

Dad went on chattering to himself as he stirred the pot of chili on the stove. Making chili wasn't that interesting. I could tell Dad was trying to act nonchalant. He didn't want to give me a reason to wonder who was on the other end of that conversation. But I did. Why didn't Dad want to discuss it? And what could he be hiding?

"How about going bowling tonight, Satch? We haven't done that in ages."

"Sure." I tried to muster some enthusiasm, but my mind was still playing back that woman's voice. Was she someone I knew? There was something spooky about her calling me by name.

After dinner we headed across town to the bowling alley. The lanes were crowded. Dad and I stood around waiting our turn, when an over-friendly voice leaped out at us. "Sid, how are ya?" A big, burly man slapped Dad on the back.

"John, good to see ya," Dad answered.

"And this must be the chip off the old block." The man gave me a slap on the back, too. It sent me flying about three feet.

Politely, Dad started introductions. "John, this is my boy, Satch." Dad turned to me. "Satch, this is John Horvath. We work together at the office."

With that, the stranger grabbed my hand, squeezed it into clay, and vibrated my whole body up and down like a jackhammer. "How do you do, Satch?"

31

"Nice to meet you, sir," I answered. How could I say something like that, when this elephant had practically turned me into mashed potatoes? I should have returned his greeting with a karate chop.

"No Barb tonight?" the stranger nudged Dad in the side.

Barb? Was that the voice on the phone? Perhaps this creature wasn't so bad after all. Maybe he had some information.

"Ah, no, just the two of us tonight," Dad mumbled. He started shifting his weight from foot to foot. Whoever this character was, he was making Dad very nervous. "Better check our lane assignment. We don't want to miss our turn. Excuse us, John."

Dad whisked me away. He didn't want to check any lane assignment. He obviously wanted to get away from that man and any more questions about Barb whoever-she-was.

Even though Mom and Dad were divorced, Dad and I had always been close. We'd always been able to talk. Suddenly, I felt like an outsider in Dad's life. There was something Dad didn't want me to know. It wasn't my imagination.

We bowled three lousy games.

Saturday morning snow greeted us. I sat on the couch staring at the flakes hitting the glass doors. They melted, then wiggled downward in a hundred different pathways to reach the bottom.

"Well, Satch, looks like tennis is out for today,"

Dad joked. "Any ideas?"

Yeah . . . I'd like to talk. In the old days we shared things, like real pals do. Why was his life suddenly a secret? I mumbled an answer, "Whatever you want."

Silence filled the room. The snowflakes just kept on melting and wiggling down the glass.

Dad finally spoke, "Satch, what's the matter? Something wrong?"

How could he not know? He was the one pushing me out of his life. I could feel tears starting to swell up in my eyes. I couldn't act like a baby. I had to let the question out before my brain exploded. "Who's Barb?"

"Oh, oh. So that's what's bothering you." Dad smiled. He sat down next to me on the couch.

"Barb is a woman I'm dating," he started.

"Why don't you want me to know about her?"

He stammered, "I just thought you'd be uncomfortable."

"Da-ad, I'm not exactly three years old. I understand what *divorced* means."

"Satch, I know that. I just didn't want to complicate your life."

"Complicate?"

"Satch, you're a terrific kid, but you've had a lot of changes in the last two years. You don't need more."

"Changes? What's going to happen? Are you going to get married?" My stomach was on a roller coaster.

33

"No," Dad stated firmly. "That's just what I'm talking about. You don't need to think every woman I date is going to become your stepmother. That's why I didn't think you should know."

"Then what is Barb to you?"

"She's someone whose company I enjoy. We haven't known each other very long. At this point, I have no idea whether more will come of it or not."

"What's her last name? Do I know her?"

"Look, I'll let you know all about her when and if there's more to tell. Agreed?"

"Agreed," I relented.

At least Dad told me most of the truth. I didn't feel pushed out of his life anymore, just set on the sidelines.

5
Put in Charge

Dad dropped me off at church on Sunday morning. He didn't stay—as usual. Mom would bring me home with her after church. That way they didn't have to see each other. I'm used to it now, but I still hate carrying a duffel bag full of dirty clothes to Sunday school.

I strolled into my group's classroom. Lizabeth Dirkson ran up to me. "Satch, we can have the rummage sale." Lizard-breath was practically taking a bubble bath with her braces.

"Huh?" My mind was concentrating on what would leap out of her mouth next.

"Reverend Miller said we can have the rummage sale," Lizabeth repeated.

"Terrific!" My ears perked up. The message finally reached my brain.

Last Sunday our class had searched for ideas to raise money for the Lings, our adopted church family from Vietnam. The adults had taken care of the big stuff last summer, like finding them a house and car and showing them the town. In fact, the Lings had picked up English so fast and fit in so quickly, they didn't need all kinds of help like at first. They almost seemed like an everyday American family now. But we kids knew that Owosso wasn't completely home for them yet.

The Lings were desperately wanting one more thing: the rest of their relatives still in the refugee camps in Hong Kong. Hai had told me. Everyone in their family over twelve had some kind of job. Even Hai shoveled walks and delivered newspapers. But saving the money to fly fifteen people across the ocean was expensive. The Lings would never *ask* for help; we *wanted* to help. Hai was our friend. We kids had decided that friends help friends without being asked.

"Let's get organized." My mind was in a whir. There were a million things to plan. "We'll need lots of junk to sell. Everyone check at home about getting rid of old clothes, toys, even furniture."

"My grandma has lots of stuff, too," one kid volunteered.

"My aunt would love to get rid of this old couch in her basement. My uncle thinks it's some kind of treasure, but my aunt wants someone to haul it away so she can put her basket-weaving supplies in that room."

"Hey," I interrupted, "we don't need details. We just need junk, so any way you can get the stuff is all right by me."

Lizabeth spoke up, "We could ask the kids at Redeemer to join us, since their church is the co-sponsor for the Ling family. I know Marcie would want to help."

Good old Marcie. She would not only want to help, she would want to run the whole show.

"What do you think?" Lizabeth asked again.

"I don't know," I tried to stall.

"Spinner goes to Redeemer, doesn't he?" Lizabeth added.

"Well—" I knew I was falling into a trap.

"You said we need more stuff and any way we can get it is all right by you," Lizabeth reminded me.

"Yeah," the group cheered.

Tied up in my very own words. What a sneaky thing to do. I would just have to put up with Motormouth Marcie. No way was I gonna convince anyone that more profit wasn't a good idea, not after my any-way-you-can-get-the-stuff-is-all-right-by-me speech.

Reverend Miller stepped into the room. "I hear you guys are going into the used-car business," he joked. Reverend Miller was our pastor. He was there to help, but he liked to let us make the decisions. Once in a while we flubbed up by doing something stupid, but he had a way of making

37

people feel good about mistakes. He'd say, "Even a bad choice can be a good choice, if you learn from it." Then he'd smile and chuckle, "That's why I'm so smart."

He nodded, "Well, what are we waiting for? Who's in charge?"

"Satch. I think it should be Satch. After all, it was his idea to help the Lings," Lizabeth suggested.

Man, I never thought I would live to see the day Lizard-breath Lizabeth would want me in charge.

"She's right," the rest agreed.

So in charge I was.

"OK, Satch, where do we start?" Reverend Miller waited attentively.

"Uh, I guess we need to set a date first," I hesitated.

"Good idea," Reverend Miller complimented. He pulled out his pocket calendar. "How much time do you think you need? Two weeks? Two months? Two years?"

"Somewhere in that range," I joked back.

"Let's see when the church basement is available," he mumbled to himself.

I glanced over Reverend Miller's shoulder. I spotted the first week of March.

"I think report cards come out then," I said pointing to the calendar. "That means the teachers will have conferences with parents, and we won't be in school. We could run the sale on Thursday, Friday, and Saturday. Whatta ya think?"

"I think you are a terrific leader. That's exceptional planning," Reverend Miller responded. "I'll put it on the church timetable right away."

I was starting to get the hang of being in charge. It wasn't bad. My mind was clicking now. "We'll need publicity. Posters, newspaper ads, and notices in the church bulletin."

"My dad works at the newspaper. I can ask him about putting an ad in the paper the week before," a fifth grader volunteered.

"My mother helps in the church office. I'll ask her to put the information in the bulletin," another kid announced.

Being the boss was super. all I had to do was give orders. I could live with that. Everyone else did the work.

"Now for posters," I continued. "What about making them next week in class?"

"I'm terrible at spacing letters," complained a fourth grader.

"That's OK," Lizabeth smiled. "I'll help you. Maybe I can space the letters out in pencil and you can color them in with marking pen. How's that?"

"Oh, thanks," sighed the girl.

Without knowing it, Lizabeth had given me an idea. I explained, "We'll set up an assembly line. Each kid will do the same part on every poster and pass it on to the next person in line. That way, each of us will only have to learn how to do one part. We'll have twenty posters done in no time flat."

"Great organizing, Satch," Reverend Miller complimented me again.

"We'd like to ask the kids from Redeemer to join us if they're interested. Do you think you could contact Pastor Jeffries to see if it's OK?" I asked.

"Sure. No problem."

"OK. One last thing before we're done today. We need to inventory the poster board and markers available in the art closet, reserve those materials for next week, and place an order for additional supplies through the church secretary. Anyone want to take responsibility for that?"

Lizabeth's hand raised timidly.

"OK, it's yours. Thanks."

Lizabeth marched off to the supply room like a robot. This was unreal. I was actually masterminding this whole operation. There was nothing to this being the boss stuff. Even the girls were following orders.

6
The Veiled
Valentine Strikes

Monday morning arrived. The first day of the Veiled Valentine game was to begin. I snuck over to Lizabeth's desk and left some newly sharpened pencils. She didn't seem to notice. Mysteriously, I found some Hubba Bubba Bubble Gum at my desk when I returned. The note attached said:

> Chew away to your heart's delight,
> Bet you won't guess me before Thursday night.
> From your Veiled Valentine

Hmm, catchy little note. Who could it be? Good taste in gum. How could he know grape was my favorite flavor? Maybe this mystical valentine game wouldn't be so bad after all.

41

On Tuesday, my sister Lisa let me have some old hair ribbons attached to barrettes. I crept over to Lizabeth's valentine holder and dropped them in. Lizabeth must have found them, because a half hour later she had them in her hair.

When the class returned from the gym, a rolled paper tube was lying on my desk. Attached to it was a note:

> A great guy like you
> Can be a superhero, too.
> Your VV

Looked interesting. I peeled it open. Wow! A poster of Brad Van Pelt. Autographed even! He was just about the most famous person ever to live in little old Owosso, Michigan. A real live professional football player. My VV was really neat, whoever he was. What astounding taste!

"I know who your secret valentine is," Marcie hummed. "La, la, la-la." She jabbed me with the corner of her math book to make certain I was paying attention. "La, la, la-la."

It was difficult to figure out when Marcie was telling the truth. She'd do almost anything to avoid story problems. And bugging me was a full-time occupation for her.

"La, la, la-la," she singsonged away. "You'll be surprised, *Siiidney*."

"Oh, you're just jealous because your valentine has left you nothing but stones, when he should have left you something you needed, like a brain."

Marcie maintained her cool. She just hummed

42

away, "La, la, la-la." She paid no attention to my witty remark. "You'll be surprised. And I'm not going to tell you. I should help out the underprivileged, though, so I will give you just one little clue: *She's* a very clever person."

She? Did Marcie really know something? Naw. No girl could come up with grape Hubba Bubba and an autographed football poster. Nope. Marcie was just trying to torment me with this she's-a-very-clever-person routine.

On Wednesday I left Lizabeth a few candy hearts, the kind with sayings on them. I had checked the hearts over first and gave her the ones that said stuff like, "See ya" or "Dig it" or "Big deal." I ate all the hearts that said, "Loving you, babe" or "You send me" and stuff like that. I didn't want Lizabeth to find a mushy one and think I liked her or something dumb like that.

When I left the candy, I found a note addressed to me:

> To Lizabeth's Veiled Valentine,
> You are very nice. Thank you for the new pencils and the pretty hair ribbons.
> From,
> Lizabeth

My own secret valentine visited me on Wednesday. I ripped open the envelope on my desk. Out fell a ticket to Saturday night's high school basketball game. Unbelievable! This Veiled Valentine of mine must be a mind reader. How did he know I loved basketball? A note slid out of the envelope:

43

Dribble, rebound, shoot, or pass.

Mister, you're the best in the class.

Your VV

Then it hit me. Zowie! Marcie's uncle was a coach at the high school. Could Motormouth Marcie be my VV? No, please, don't let it be.

"Spinner, it's just too coincidental. It has to be Marcie. She's setting me up."

"Come on, Satch. Marcie isn't that smart."

"But the poster. Her uncle knows Brad Van Pelt. He was his coach. And the ticket. That proves it. Her uncle probably gave her the ticket. In fact, Marcie probably has it rigged so she'll sit beside me. She may even kidnap me. Save me, Spinner."

"Calm down, Satch," Spinner laughed. "Let me see that ticket." He grabbed it out of my hand to inspect it. "Don't worry. This ticket isn't numbered. You can sit anywhere."

"Hey, sitting on the opposite side of the gym and cheering for the other team isn't far enough away from that mouth."

"Come on, you're worried about nothing. That ticket wasn't free. Marcie wouldn't spend real money on you," Spinner reasoned.

"Motormouth Marcie would spend a million dollars if she thought she could make a fool out of me." Yep, Marcie was fattening me up for the kill. That was her strategy, and I had been falling for it.

Thursday arrived. I was running out of ideas for Lizabeth. I found some old stickers in my desk drawer. They'd do. She could stick them on a notebook or better yet, across Motormouth Marcie's lips. I delivered the stickers as the class dismissed for lunch.

When we came back, my desk had a strange bottle sitting on it. Oh, yuck! After-shave lotion. *Musk for the He-Man* was taped on the bottle's label. A note stuck to my desk read:

Use a big FIST-A-FULL
And you'll be IRRE-SIST-IBLE.
Saturday night I'll be in line,
To claim my ever-lovin' valentine.
    Your VV

My eyes lifted off the paper. The whole class had been snickering while watching me read. How could Marcie write this goop?

Miss Hepburn smiled and quieted down the group. "Let's take out our math books, please."

Marcie poked me again with her favorite book. "*Siiidney*, any plans for Saturday night? My uncle says it's going to be a good one."

Knock it off, Marcie. I don't think it's cute. You're not fooling me.

"Satch," Miss Hepburn called, "do you feel OK?"

"I'm fine," I mumbled. *I just look green because this Veiled Vulcher behind me is waiting to collect the pieces after she rips me into shreds with words.*

45

7
The Unveiling

Friday arrived. In the morning we did our regular schoolwork. Just as we were lining up to leave for lunch, the school secretary called over the PA system, "Miss Hepburn, please send Marcie Cook to the office to pick up a package from her mother."

Miss Hepburn shouted at the speaker, "Marcie is on kindergarten crossing guard duty. May I send another messenger?"

"Yes, that will be fine," the speaker answered. *Click.* The PA system was off.

"Satch, would you go to the office and pick up Marcie's package, please?"

"Sure."

What could I say? No, the bomb in the package is meant for Marcie?

I trotted down the hall. Usually doing an errand was fun, but something told me I'd better be wary since this involved Marcie. My stomach was churning.

When I reached the office, the secretary handed me the package. What could be in there? It wasn't very heavy. I strolled back toward the classroom, casually reading the note taped on the outside:

> Marcie,
> Hope this is what you need.
> Love, B.J.

Marcie always called her mother B.J. She thought she was really grown up addressing her mother by her initials. I guess her mom played along with the gag.

I laid the package on Marcie's desk and hurried to catch up with the guys in the lunch line.

"Satch," A.J. whispered, "you got your eggs ready?"

"Yeah. I stashed 'em in my locker this morning before school. What'd you do with yours?"

"Same thing," A.J. snickered.

"How we gonna spring it on 'em?" Spinner worried. "Miss Hepburn will squelch the fun if she finds out too soon."

I had thought it out a thousand times. "When she asks us what games we have planned, we'll just say the last one has to be played outside because we need lots of room. We grab our coats fast and keep

47

the eggs under cover till we hit the playground."

"Yeah, we'll pair up kids and hand them an egg before Miss Hepburn realizes what's happening," Spinner finished.

"This be blast," Hai added, trying out his new American slang. "We cream 'em." Hai's eyes danced. Even he could predict the future of The Great Egg Exchange.

"The girls will be covered," chuckled A.J.

"They can't even catch a fat old kickball. Wait till those eggs start flying." We were already cracking up inside.

We came back from lunch set to begin the party. Marcie strolled in last behind Lizabeth. The two of them were smirking at each other. Little did she know. She might embarrass me with the Veiled Valentine gag, but I'd have the last laugh. Once those eggs entered the scene, she'd be sorry.

Marcie hummed her little hum, "La, la, la-la." She sauntered by my desk. She was no doubt bursting to tell me she was the mysterious author of those dumb poems. "La, la, la-la."

"All set, folks? Let's get settled," Miss Hepburn announced.

My eyes followed Marcie to her seat. Hey, the package was gone. When did she have time to get it?

"Are you ready for this, *Siiidney?* Do you think a brain your size can figure out who's been leaving you valentines all week?"

"You haven't fooled me, Marcie. I know your

48

uncle's the basketball coach. I had it figured out ages ago."

"Why, *Siiidney*, how complimentary of you, to honor me with the astute character your secret admirer has shown. I really wish I could take credit for the shrewd methods she has exercised. But you, *Siiidney* Carlton, are quite mistaken. I respectfully congratulate the one person in this room who is even more clever than myself."

Aw, can it, Marcie. Turn off the motor. In five minutes this whole farce would be over, and we could stop this charade.

"Now, let's get started," Miss Hepburn announced. "It's time for the secret valentines to unveil themselves. We'll begin with Spinner's row. Will you please make your last delivery and reveal your identity to your Veiled Valentine?"

Some of the kids had figured out who had been making deliveries to them. But Hai about fell off his seat when he realized Spinner had been the person leaving him vitamins and a menagerie of rubber animals.

Miss Hepburn fumbled with the papers on her desk. "Will the second row continue?"

A few whoops went up when Lizabeth delivered her valentine to A.J. That clinched it. Lizabeth was the only person in the room Marcie would credit with being anywhere near as clever as she.

"And the last row? Would you please reveal your identities?" Miss Hepburn concluded.

Marcie bounded up off her chair in a flurry. She

49

rushed to the opposite side of the room. She didn't fool me. I knew she was just trying to throw me off the track by waltzing up and down the aisles.

I stood up and politely delivered my last valentine to Lizabeth. Startled, she giggled and thanked me. What was happening to me? I turned red.

I dashed back to my seat. Marcie was still parading around the room, trying to dramatize the whole situation. I sat down and put my chin in my hands, waiting for her to bring this whole ordeal to its end.

Suddenly, I felt a shadowy figure behind me. An arm reached in front of me and dropped an envelope on my desk. Huh? Marcie was still prancing around on the other side of the room. I swiveled my body around and gazed upward. A howl of laughter ignited the classroom.

"Miss Hepburn. You?"

"Surprise. Surprise." She gave me a wink.

"I never even considered—"

"I know," she chuckled. "Happy Valentine Day."

Man, did she ever put one over on me. What a trickster. Even I had to laugh. Marcie was right about one thing. Miss Hepburn was a very clever person.

The party continued. We ate. We opened valentines. We joked. We laughed again and again at Miss Hepburn's joke on me. Now it was my turn. The Great Egg Exchange was fast approaching.

"And what is the next game the entertainment

committee has planned?" Miss Hepburn asked.

"We need to go outside where there's plenty of room," I explained. I had to carry out my gag as perfectly as Miss Hepburn had carried out hers.

"Well, since it's 3:00 and we'll need our coats to go outside, let's gather our things for home now. We'll dismiss from the playground as soon as the game is over."

Hurray. The plan was progressing on schedule. She was falling right into it.

Everyone collected their things and headed out the door. A.J., Spinner, and I kept the eggs inside our jackets. Once outside, I ordered kids to find a partner and form two rows about six feet apart. Quickly, I started passing out the eggs to the kids in the left row. Miss Hepburn was just coming out the door.

"OK. People on the left, toss your egg to your partner. If it breaks, you're out." The kids made the first toss.

Miss Hepburn was buttoning her coat as she walked toward us.

Hurriedly, I kept the game moving. We'd get to the good part soon.

"People in the right line, take two giant steps backward," I ordered.

Everyone obeyed.

"Ready? Throw," I shouted.

We were sure to get some scrambled eggs on this throw. Two girls missed. Whoopee. Miraculously, the eggs were undamaged. *Hmm* . . . the snow must have softened the fall. Just lucky. Wait till they get farther apart.

"OK. People in the left line take two giant steps backward," I commanded.

Again the kids marched back.

"Ready? Throw."

This would really be a massacre. Eggs sailed through the air. A giant white missile lobbed right for Motormouth Marcie. She ducked. Oh, boy, Marcie would be pancake batter in a matter of seconds.

Crash. Huh? Her egg didn't break.

Neither did anybody else's, and plenty of them dropped. The snow wasn't that soft! We hadn't been outside long enough for the eggs to freeze, had we?

"Let me see that egg." I snatched the egg from Marcie.

The shell was cracked all right, but the egg inside was cooked. Boiled as hard as a rock. I clunked a couple more eggs together. Same thing. It would take a car crusher to smash these eggs.

I glared over at A.J. He shrugged his shoulders in disbelief. I glared at Spinner. He looked just as puzzled.

Someone had switched eggs on us. Miss Hepburn? Had she known all along? She had certainly outsmarted me with that Veiled Valentine number. Could she have pulled this off, too? She just stood there smiling as if nothing was wrong. What a cover.

"Game over, fellas?" she sighed, "I guess I missed the whole thing."

"Yeah, it's over," I answered.

She sure didn't give any clues. Was that why she took so long buttoning her coat?

Miss Hepburn went about her normal routine. "Time to collect up our things, kids," she announced. "The dismissal bell will ring any minute. We don't want anyone missing a bus."

Brrrring.

Kids scattered. Pete and A.J. clambered for their bus. Spinner, Hai, and I started walking home.

"I just can't figure it out, guys," I groaned. "How could she have known? When did she switch the eggs?"

"Hey, face it, Satch, she's one smart teacher." Spinner shook his head.

"All teachers have ten ears, Satch," Hai added.

"Fellas?" a voice behind us called. We turned to see who it was. "You forgot something."

SPLAT! SPLAT! SPLAT!

Marcie and Lizabeth landed a downpour of raw eggs on us. SPLAT! SPLAT! SPLAT!

Yuck! Egg yolk dribbled down my nose and earlobes. My hair was like yellow papier-maché. I tried to wipe the slimy goop from my mouth and eyes. It clung like Super Glue.

Hai and Spinner were covered, too. They looked like they'd come straight out of a blender.

Now I knew what was in that package Marcie's mother sent her—hard-boiled eggs. Marcie had

53

played her own version of The Great Egg Exchange and I had helped.

Poor Hai. He looked at me desperately. "I think you better off to call this American custom Egg Drop Soup."

8
The Stars Are Out Tonight

I took about a three-hour bath to clean off the egg I wore home from school Friday.

This was my weekend to be with Mom, so I had to convince her she wanted to see the basketball game Saturday night. I tried the we-can't-miss-this-terrific-game method.

"Mom, the Trojans have a great team this year. They might even win the league title."

"Title to what?" she asked innocently.

"You know, the championship."

"Oh, I see," Mom nodded her head, but she didn't really see.

Time to try the pitiful approach. I switched gears.

"Mo-om, Spinner's whole family is going. They're even taking Hai. Everyone will be there."

"Well, if it's that important to you, I suppose we can go."

Mom was a pretty good sport, considering she didn't know a thing about basketball.

As we entered the doorway, I heard a voice behind me, "Barb. Over here, Barb."

Barb? Barb who? I swung around to get a better look. A mass of heads crowded forward, none of which I recognized. Could *she* be one of those faces? I shook it from my head. Naw. I've got to stop thinking every Barb I see is Dad's girl friend.

We climbed up the bleachers to where Hai and Spinner were sitting. The rest of the Spinnellis were there, too.

Mom and Mrs. Spinnelli had become great friends since the Ling family arrived last summer. The two of them were the "neighborhood adjustment coordinators" from our two churches. Those first few weeks, Mom and Mrs. Spinnelli practically lived with the Lings. I never realized people in other parts of the world lived so differently from us. Running a washing machine, shopping at the grocery store, even using a can opener were all experiences the Lings needed explained to them.

"Hi, Satch," Mr. Spinnelli greeted me. "Think our Trojans can win tonight?"

"With that star-studded lineup, they will. I expect the other team will be blinded by the light alone."

"That's the spirit, Satch. The stars will be out tonight," Mr. Spinnelli kidded.

I started leafing through the program to find the close-up pictures of the team. "Hey, look," I leaned over toward Spinner and Hai. "There's A.J.'s brother." I pointed to the picture.

"Me see. Me see," Frankie whined.

"See? There he is," I pointed again as I held up the program for Frankie to see.

"Gimme. Gimme. I want book," Frankie ordered. He was never satisfied. He always had to have everything his way.

Luckily, Mrs. Spinnelli solved the problem. "Here, Frankie, you take my book," she soothed.

I continued looking at the Trojans' pictures. "Hai, Spinner, look. This guy's name is Larry Hepburn."

"Teacher's family?" Hai asked.

"I don't know. We'll have to ask. Maybe A.J. knows.'"

"Piiin-ner, I have to go potty," Frankie announced. "Reeeeal bad. Reeeeal bad, Pinner." He wiggled back and forth, making us all very nervous. Yep, Frankie would definitely get his own way again. Never negotiate when Frankie has to go to the bathroom.

"Come on, guys. Let's go," Spinner complained.

The three of us hopped off the edge of the bleachers to avoid crawling over people. We were up about ten rows, too high for Frankie to jump by himself.

57

"Jump, Frankie. I'll catch ya." Spinner held out his arms.

"Whee!" Frankie leaped into the air and landed in Spinner's arms.

"Do it again. I like Superman," Frankie commanded.

Hmm . . . I thought this superhero had to go to the bathroom.

"Come on, Frankie," Spinner said firmly.

"No. Frankie play Superman."

"Come on, you little monster. I'm leaving." Spinner started to walk away.

"Frankie play Superman," he screamed louder than the cheering fans.

I tried coaxing him, "Frankie, we'll play Superman after we go to the bathroom."

"NO! FRANKIE PLAY SUPERMAN, NOW!" Once more Frankie anchored his feet on the floor ready to do battle in front of an audience.

I stepped up to Frankie and whispered in his ear, "Frankie, even Superman has to go to the bathroom."

Guess he never thought about that. Frankie spread out his arms and zoomed toward the bathrooms.

Afterwards, we crawled through the crowd of people back to our seats, but not before stumbling over Motormouth Marcie. It didn't take her any time at all to start her engine.

"Well, hello, hello, hello, if it isn't the three wise crackers. Been cracking any jokes at the chicken farm lately?" she jeered.

I twisted my face back at her. I could never think of a comeback to top Marcie's. How could she always have something smart on the tip of her tongue? She just opened her mouth and out it poured.

I sat down and tried to watch the game. Owosso's Trojans were out in front.

"Popcorn. I want popcorn," Frankie ordered.

"Later," Spinner said, still trying to watch the game.

"No. Popcorn now."

"Mo-om," Spinner looked over at Mrs. Spinnelli.

"Would you, honey?" she pleaded. "We really can't get out as easily as you fellas." She dug into her purse and dangled money in front of our faces. "Here's some extra. You three can get yourselves a treat, too."

It didn't look like such a hard job after all. The three of us hopped down the edge of the bleachers again. Frankie beamed. He was ready to play Superman.

"Whee. Superman." Frankie leaped off the edge so quickly. I barely had time to reach out and catch him.

"Superman. Again. Again," Frankie sang out.

"Come on, Frankie. Let's go," Spinner ordered.

"No. Frankie play Superman."

"Look, Superman is gonna get creamed with Kryptonite if he doesn't get a move on," Spinner threatened.

59

"NO! FRANKIE PLAY SUPERMAN!"

Frankie was ready to do battle. Threats only made him rise to the challenge. The only way to outfox Frankie was to make him think *he* was making the decision.

"Hey, Frankie. Superman loves popcorn. Hot, buttery popcorn. *Ummm*," I dramatized.

"Zoooom." Frankie zipped over to the concession stand at warp speed.

I was so busy watching Frankie, I practically fell over when I heard a familiar voice talking to me. "Hello there, valentine. Enjoying the game?"

"Miss Hepburn!" I yelled, still startled.

"What's that wonderful aroma I smell? Could it be Fist-a-full After-shave Lotion?" she kidded.

What a tease. She knew I wouldn't wear that stinky stuff.

"What are you doing here?" Spinner asked.

"Just helping out the Sports Booster Club. My brother's on the basketball team."

"Surprise to see you," Hai added.

"What can I sell ya, fellas?" Miss Hepburn smiled.

"Zoom!" Frankie flew between us. "Suuuuperman."

"How about a leash?" I suggested.

Miss Hepburn winked. She always got my jokes. Guess that's why she was my favorite teacher.

"Excuse me, Barb," another worker interrupted, "Could you help me lift . . ."

Barb? There's that name again. Could she be?

60

Dad wouldn't date my teacher, would he? Naw. It's just a coincidence. I shook it from my mind. Spinner asked me something. I nodded. *Barb? Was she the voice on the phone who seemed to know me?*

"We'll have four popcorns and four Cokes," Spinner spoke up.

Miss Hepburn handed us the stuff. In a daze, I headed back up the bleachers with the group.

Marcie's motor snapped me to attention, "*Siiidney,* we came here to watch a basketball game, not play musical chairs. Remember? Can you figure that much out? Or maybe you can't. I'll give you a clue. The teams each try to put the ball through that hoop out there."

Put it in reverse, Marcie.

I continued climbing the bleachers to my seat.

The Trojans barely had time to sink a basket before Frankie Spinnelli decided it was time to take his act on the road again.

"Satch, buddy, I gotta go potty."

"You just went."

"I gotta go again."

"How could you?"

"Just lucky." Frankie grinned dangerously.

I sighed, "OK. OK. I'll take you." It would be easier to just get it over with. Maybe we could watch the game in peace afterward. "Come on."

I jumped off the edge of the bleachers. *Thud.* I was just coming out of my squatting position to prepare for Frankie's jump when I heard—

"Wheee. Super—'"
Crash.
Something flattened me.
Clunk.
My head hit the floor. Stars danced in front of my eyes. Then everything went black.

I don't know how long my lights were out, but people tell me I was unconscious about five minutes. My mother said it was forever.

Frankie came out of it in great shape. In fact, when I finally came to, he was proudly taking full credit, saying, "See, I told you. Frankie Superman. Superman saved Satch."

9
Me? Talented?

Mom immediately checked me over for signs of a concussion. She kept staring into my eyes and asking, "Honey, are you sure you don't feel sick to your stomach?"

"Mom, I'm fine," I protested. Everyone was staring at me like I had two heads or something.

But being a mother, Mom insisted, "I really would feel better if we went to the emergency room for X rays."

I really would feel better if those people would stop glaring at me and start watching the basketball game.

Mom won out. Off to the hospital we went. We sat for two boring hours while some doctor took pictures of my skull, told her I was fine, and charged her a whopping fee. Why can't mothers just take your word when you tell them you're OK?

Sunday morning we headed out for church early. Reverend Miller was scurrying around the classroom area.

"Howdy, Satch," he greeted me. "Aren't you the early bird this morning."

"Just wanted to get the poster production line organized before everyone arrives."

"Ah, the workings of a great intellect," Reverend Miller joked. "Satch, it's good to see you use your God-given talents."

Talent? Me? I always knew I was smart, but I never really considered it a God-given talent. Talent was something like singing or dancing or drawing.

"Pastor Jeffries is sending the kids from Redeemer over here today. He thought maybe you'd like to explain your rummage sale ideas to them in person."

"Oh. That sounds good. Maybe we'll even have time to make some posters together if they go for the project."

"The supplies you ordered are in the art closet. Gotta go, kiddo. See ya later." Reverend Miller dashed off.

"Thanks," I called out.

I headed for the closet to unload the supplies. *Hmm* . . . markers, rulers, poster board. Yep, it's all there. Hey, what was this package of letters?

64

"Hi, Satch," Lizabeth peered around the corner.

"Oh, hi."

"Need some help?" she offered.

"Yeah, I guess so. I was just getting things organized," I answered cautiously.

"I hope I ordered the right things," Lizabeth said nervously. "I also found some patterns for tracing letters. I thought it might help some of the kids who don't know how to make posters very well."

"We could try them out," I nodded.

Man, Lizabeth was actually worried I wouldn't like her ideas.

"Why don't we make a sample poster?" I suggested.

"OK."

Lizabeth and I hauled the materials to the worktables. In pencil Lizabeth spaced the giant letters: BENEFIT RUMMAGE SALE. Hey, she was good. Underneath in smaller letters, she spaced: MARCH 6, 7, 8 from 9:00 a.m. to 4:00 p.m. Lizabeth was going to town. She added the church location. Then she drew pictures of coats, shorts, tennis rackets, bicycles, chairs, everything. Lizabeth was a pro. It looked fantastic.

"What do you think?" Lizabeth asked hesitantly, holding up her poster.

"It's terrific. Man, can you ever draw."

Talk about talent. I never knew Lizabeth was an artist.

"If the kids at Redeemer decide to help, I can center their names right here next to ours." Lizabeth pointed to the lower half of the poster.

"Yeah, good idea." Who was I to question Picasso.

Kids started arriving and admiring the poster. "Hey, don't look at me." I smiled. "Lizabeth's the designer."

Lizabeth blushed. I never realized how shy she was. I guess Marcie had always overshadowed her.

Before long, a van filled with kids entered the parking lot. They were obviously the group from Redeemer. I could see Spinner hanging out the window. They piled out. Great, there was Marcie. And with her was her mother. I guess she must have been the Sunday school teacher.

I could hear Mrs. Cook giving instructions: "Let us remember, we are guests. I expect you to act accordingly."

I wondered if she gives orders to everyone like Marcie does?

The kids filed into our youth room. Most of them I knew. A few, I didn't.

"Hi, Satch," Mrs. Cook greeted me politely. "Pastor Jeffries said you have some great ideas for helping the Lings. I haven't told the kids anything yet. I thought *you'd* like to do that."

Man, that was a surprise. Marcie always had to be the one to blab everything.

"Thank you, Mrs. Cook."

"Oh, Satch, you can call me B.J.," she smiled.

Mrs. Cook was certainly different from that venomous creature she had for a daughter.

I tried to get the meeting started. "Now that everyone has found a seat, could I have your attention, please?"

The room quieted down.

"We have invited you here to discuss the possibility of your joining us in our Benefit Rummage Sale. We hope to raise enough money to buy airline tickets for the Lings' relatives still living in Hong Kong. Maybe with our profits all the Lings will make it to America."

As usual, Marcie interrupted, "Why is Hai's family in Hong Kong? I thought they were from Vietnam."

I went on to explain, "When the war ended, thousands of people had to flee their homes or risk being killed. Many people escaped by boat, including the Lings. Lots of the refugees landed in Hong Kong. But the city didn't know what to do with all these homeless people. They were shoved into detention camps. That's about like a jail. The people are alive, but basically they still have no freedom. Hai's family waited three years in a detention camp for our churches to adopt them."

Moans rose up around the room.

I continued, "We've done a lot to help the Lings. We can be very proud of that. But there's still more work to be done. These people need us. So what do you say?"

"Yeah." A cheer rang out.

The group was sold. Everyone started talking at once. "My mother has this old fur coat that should bring in a lot of money. . . ."

"My dad has an exercise bike he wants to get rid of. . . ."

"We've had lots of rummage sales at my house. I know exactly how to price things and how to ring up the sales." That was Marcie trying to be a big shot already.

I raised my hand for control, "Look, we need everyone's help. There's plenty of work, so spread out. I'll pass around these schedules for work details. Sign up for the times you can help. In the meantime, go through all the closets and garages you can find. Bring your things to the church basement Wednesday, March 5th, right after school."

Heads nodded in agreement.

"OK. Let's get to those posters, team."

Man, Lizabeth had been working away during all that talking. She had completed three sample posters. We set up three production squads. We were in business. I was on top of the world.

Reverend Miller came up and patted me on the shoulder, "Satch, great presentation. Great planning, too."

"Thanks." I didn't want to sound conceited, but I knew my genius organizational mind had done it again.

Reverend Miller continued, "I'm proud to see you using your leadership ability in a constructive way, Satch. Lots of people talk about loving their fellow man, but it's not always easy to live up to that principle in our daily lives."

Wow, he almost made me out to be a martyr. I only wanted to help my friend Hai.

Spinner came up and grabbed my arm, "How's your head today.?"

"Oh, I'm fine. The doctor just took a couple X rays. That's all. You know mothers. They're just worrywarts."

"Well, Frankie may have had his last flying lesson."

"I didn't think Frankie was hurt. What happened?"

"I told him Superman couldn't leap off any more tall buildings, that's why he broke out in chicken pox this morning."

10
The Secret Code

The spring thaw had begun. Except for a few dirty patches, all the snow had melted.

Brrrring. Spinner phoned before school started. "A.J. called. He wants you, me, and Hai to come over after school on our bikes. He says they have a new bike trail through the woods."

"Sounds neat. Hang on." I covered the phone. "Mom, can I ride over to A.J.'s after school?"

"I suppose," Mom consented. "Just be home by dinner."

I uncovered the receiver. "We're on. Meet ya in ten minutes at the corner."

I shoved down some Cheerios and jumped on my bike. Just as I was about to streak out of the driveway, Mom yelled out the window, "Satch, you forgot your spring jacket."

"Aw, Mom, it's going to be 100° this afternoon."

"Aren't you exaggerating just a little, Satch?"

"I'll fry right on the sidewalk," I complained.

Mom didn't appreciate my humor. She stuck to her order. "Wear a jacket. It's chilly this morning. You know how unpredictable this Michigan weather is. It's best to be prepared."

"Yeah, yeah," I mumbled.

"If it warms up this afternoon, take the jacket off and tie the sleeves around your waist."

Sure. Great idea. Then I would look like I was wearing half a skirt.

It was useless to argue. I grabbed my jacket and made tracks. Mom was such a worrywart.

I rounded Oliver Street to pick up Spinner and Hai. Two bicycles were coming my way, probably the guys. With the sun right behind them, all I could make out were their silhouettes. I stopped and waited.

"Siiidney, haven't you figured out how to ride a bike, yet?" Instantly, I knew the silhouettes weren't the guys. There's only one person in the world who dares to call me *Siiidney*.

"Now that my little sister Mandy is done with her training wheels, you might be able to borrow them if you say pretty please with sugar on it."

Lizabeth spoke up, "Are you OK, Satch? Is something wrong with your bike?"

"I'm fine. I'm just waiting for Spinner and Hai," I

answered. Actually, Lizabeth wasn't so bad. She had learned to talk without spitting in all directions because of her braces.

Spinner and Hai were waving in the distance as they approached me. Marcie made her getaway with one last insult, "Now that your baby-sitters have arrived, I suppose Lizabeth and I can safely leave you."

"What was that all about?" Spinner questioned.

"Oh, Marcie was just her usual, charming self."

"You didn't tell her about the bike trail, did you?"

"Do you think I'm crazy?"

Hai laughed, "She make you plenty mad to do foolish things."

"Well, you're right there. Marcie could make a rattlesnake bite himself."

When we arrived at school, Pete and A.J. were already locking their bikes to the rack.

I had to warn them. "Look, guys. Marcie's on the prowl. She's determined to stick her mouth into our business. I bet she even follows us after school to find out what we're doing."

"Let's scatter in different directions," A.J. suggested.

The school bell rang, and we headed toward the open doors. Spinner spoke up. "We'll make plans at recess."

"Gotcha," we nodded.

We filed into the classroom. Miss Hepburn greeted us with her usual Monday morning smile.

Did she look at me differently from the rest of the kids? I couldn't tell. I took my seat. What if she was Dad's Barb? Maybe that's why she spent all that money on me for the Veiled Valentine game? Could she be trying to make me like her in case she ended up marrying Dad? *Hmm . . .* maybe it wouldn't be so bad. She was a lot of fun. But what would the guys say? Worse yet, what would Motormouth Marcie say?

I could just hear that motor race: "Students of Roosevelt School, I ask you to see this worthless creature for what he truly is. Those A's we've had shoved in our faces all year long are not the work of a mathematical genius. They are the shrewd methods of a maniacal weasel. He's a fraud. While we've been slaving away diagraming sentences and converting miles to kilometers, this little sneak thief has been consorting with the enemy. He has willfully accepted free answers from the teacher's manual in order that she may win his approval to date his father."

The class would shriek in horror. "I ask you, fellow classmates, are we going to stand idly by and watch this?"

"NO, NO," the hypnotized crowd would answer.

"It's time that justice was served."

"JUSTICE. JUSTICE. WE WANT JUSTICE." The crowd would soon be rioting.

And before I could explain, Marcie would have me strung up the flagpole, by my toenails, yet.

"Yeow," I jumped and shouted.

73

"Satch?" Miss Hepburn broke in. "Earth to Satch. Do you read me, over?"

The class laughed.

"Are you back with us, Satch?" Miss Hepburn joked.

"Oh, yeah," I stammered.

"Would you please solve problem number five for us?"

"Sure."

I wished she would just yell at me for not paying attention. Kids would be sure to notice that she was always nice to me, even when I was goofing off. Didn't she know that teachers were supposed to yell at kids?

Recess arrived, finally. It was time to plot strategy with the guys. "How about sending coded messages?" A.J. suggested. He was good at undercover work.

"Like what?" Spinner asked skeptically.

"When you want to tell me something, just write it down using the letter of the alphabet that comes after the real letter you mean."

"Sort of like B stands for A and K stands for J?"

"Right."

"Hey, that's cool. The girls will never figure that out. They've barely mastered pig Latin."

In social studies class I composed the first coded note to Spinner. It said, "You take Washington Street and I'll take Park Street. Meet you at Pete's corner. Beware of the MOUTH." The note looked like this:

74

Zpv ublf Xbtijohupo Tusffu boe J'mm ublf
Qbsl Tusffu. Nffu zpv bu Qfuf't dpsofs. Cfxbsf
pg uif NPVUI.

"What's going on, *Siiidney*? That's not social
studies." Marcie was quick to peer over my
shoulder.

"I'm practicing Russian in my spare time. See?" I
held up the coded note. Marcie's jaw dropped.
There was no way she could decipher this.

I went up to the front of the room to sharpen my
pencil and dropped the note into Spinner's lap. In
no time at all, Spinner sent me a reply:

Hppe qmbo. Qfuf boe B.K. xjmm ublf Ibj xjui
uifn boe ifbe pvu Ijdlpsz Spbe. Cfxbsf pg uif
NPVUI.

I put down my map of the Rocky Mountain states
and set to work decoding Spinner's message. *Hmm*
. . . H means G. PP means OO. Ah. First word
"Good." I wrote it above Spinner's letters. I
continued until I had figured out, "Good plan. Pete
and A.J. will—"

"*Siiidney* Carlton, if you think I believe you
about practicing Russian, you've got oatmeal between your ears. You guys are up to something. Let
me see that." She reached for Spinner's note.

I snatched it away just in time. With half the
words decoded, she might figure out the rest. I
stuffed it in my mouth. Yuck! How on earth do
spies swallow their secrets?

In a flash Miss Hepburn stood over my desk. She
didn't say a word. She just gave me a cough-it-up-

or-else look. Then she held out her hand.

"Um?" I choked out my innocent response.

She didn't fall for it. She just glared at me harder with her do-you-really-want-me-to-crawl-in-there-and-get-it-myself look.

I opened my mouth and pulled out the note. Delicately, she carried it to her desk using only the tips of her fingernails.

Man, was I gonna get it now. Miss Hepburn liked to joke around, but assignments were assignments and they'd better be given first priority. I could see her staring at me from across the room. What would she do? She was so unpredictable.

Lunchtime came. Still no punishment. The guys crowded around me in the lunch line.

"What did Miss Hepburn do to you?" Hai asked.

"I'll probably get the guillotine," I groaned.

"Naw, she wasn't mad," Spinner spoke up. "She could hardly keep from laughing when you had that note stashed in your mouth."

"Yeah, Satch. She likes you. She won't do anything," A.J. commented.

Oh, no. What if I *was* getting special treatment? What if she *was* Dad's girl friend and she *was* trying to win me over? What if the guys were suspicious? I almost wanted after-school cleanup detail.

All afternoon I stared at my English book. *Please, please, punish me. Show me you hate me. Show everyone you hate me.*

Finally, just before afternoon recess was about to start, Miss Hepburn called me up to her desk.

Yippee! I was gonna get chewed out. And it would be in front of the whole class. Now, no one would suspect. This would be great.

Instead, Miss Hepburn handed me a note and sent me outside with the rest of the class. Huh? She wasn't supposed to do that.

"What's the note say? What's it say?" the guys demanded.

"It's not in English," I moaned.

A.J. grabbed the note and cracked up. "Hey, what a joker. She used our very own code to send you a message, Satch."

He held it up for everyone to see:

Tbwf zpvs opuft gps uif bgufs tdippm ipvs, Ps zpv'mm gjoe zpvstfmg mpdlfe jo MPOEPO UPXFS. (Uibu't Spptfwfmu Tdippm efufoujpo jo dbtf zpv epo'u hfu nz esjgu.) Cfxbsf pg uif CJH CVSO.

It took us all recess period to translate but we finally came out with:

Save your notes for the after-school hour, or you'll find yourself locked in LONDON TOWER. (That's Roosevelt School detention in case you don't get my drift.) Beware of the BIG BURN.

"See, I told you," A.J. said confidently. "All you got was a warning. Miss Hepburn likes you, Satch."

Didn't I know. What did I have to do to make her mad? What was the real message in that secret code?

11
The Hideout

After school the five of us split to meet at Pete's corner. We were taking no chances with any of the girls following us. Pete and A.J. lived in one of the new subdivisions out of town. All kinds of leftover building supplies were lying around on the empty lots.

"Follow me," ordered A.J. He headed deep into the woods. "Watch me do this figure eight." A.J. spun off at top speed.

"And look at me take this three-foot ramp," shouted Pete.

Wow! The course looked like pros had laid it out. Pete and A.J. whipped around the curves with expertise. Spinner, Hai, and I followed. We zoomed in and out of trees and up and down the berms.

"Hey," Spinner called, resting for a time on the sidelines, "if we move this rock out of here, we can add a whole new section to the trail."

We pushed and twisted and pried. We were plenty exhausted, but we finally managed to move the rock out of the way. Unfortunately, we had created another problem, a giant three-foot hole.

"Wait," I said, thinking out loud, "let's not fill it in. Let's dig it out. We can put some of these boards across the top and make a hideout."

"Yeah," the guys agreed.

Ideas came pouring out from everyone.

"We could cover the boards with this tar paper."

"And we could put dirt over the tar paper so no one would think anything special was even here."

"Those long branches over there could conceal the opening."

"What a fantastic clubhouse."

We all raced home for shovels and saws. This would be the neatest secret hideout in history.

Riding across town with a shovel on my handlebars wasn't exactly easy. People gave me some pretty strange looks when they passed me, but I didn't care.

For the next three days, the five of us met every day after school at the secret hideout. And the best part was, the girls had no idea what was going on. We had certainly outsmarted them.

Friday morning I scurried to get dressed for

school. Today the guys would have extra time at the hideout. Maybe we could even expand the hideout to a tunnel.

"Satch, must you wear those old jeans to school?" Mom complained.

"Mom, you don't want me to wreck any good ones, do you? The guys and I are working on a project. It's pretty dirty."

"But the side pocket is torn. It looks so shabby. Why don't you at least let me stitch it up?"

"Aw, Mom, I'll be late. It's OK."

Mom sighed.

I ran out the door before she could remind me to wear a jacket in her famous "best to be prepared" speech.

When I reached school, I locked my bike at the rack. I sat on a swing waiting for the guys to arrive.

"*Siiidney*, be careful on that swing. We wouldn't want to see you hurt yourself. When your baby-sitters come, maybe they'll give you a little push."

"Aw, bug off, Marcie." I tried to ignore her.

"Or maybe you can play in the sandbox while you wait. Poor baby, he probably left his shovel in A.J.'s playpen."

"Just stay out of our business."

"Well, what else could an intelligent person assume if they saw you riding all over town with a shovel on your bicycle handlebars?"

"Assume we're digging graves—and our next order is YOURS!"

There! I finally thought of a comeback to one of

Marcie's insults. I started pumping the swing just to show her I didn't have to sit still and take her snide comments anymore.

Marcie started her swing going, too.

I went higher.

She went higher.

I pumped harder.

She pumped harder.

I went still higher. The wind was racing against my face like a hurricane. I'd show her. She was too chicken to swing as high as me. She'd be afraid of flipping over the bar.

Marcie took the dare. She swung higher and higher, matching my speed.

Why did this beast always plague me?

I wouldn't let her beat me. Never, I was calling the shots. And I'd win. *I bet she wouldn't dare jump out of the swing while we're going fifty miles an hour. I'll leap out like I have wings on my feet. With this momentum, I'll sail clear over to the slide. Marcie's jaw will drop. Naw, she's too cowardly to try my flying trapeze act.*

I tucked my legs under the swing to build up speed. I gritted my teeth. My eyes were focused straight ahead. Three was the magic number. Inside myself I counted to the rhythm of the swing. Back. And forth. Back. And forth. Back. And one. Back. And two. Back. And THREE. Out I catapulted like I was being shot out of a cannon.

Rrrrrip! The side pocket of my jeans caught on the chain of the swing. As I plummeted through the air, I was shredding my pants into miles and miles of designer Red Cross bandages. By the time I landed, I was wearing nothing but a waistband and kneepads. I bent down and picked up the remains of my jeans. Not one piece was big enough to use as even a dustrag.

Ah! Where could I hide? I couldn't run into the office with just underwear on. Everyone was staring. *Ah!* What if Miss Hepburn saw me? Home. I had to get home. If only I'd worn a jacket to wrap around my bare legs.

I managed to convince my paralyzed legs to run over to the bike rack, but they obeyed only in slow motion. I had to sprint out of there. *Ah!* My bike was locked. What birdbrain locked it? I fumbled with the combination. *Thirty-two right. Turn. Turn. Fifteen left. Turn. Turn. Ah! I meant thirty-two left. Turn. Turn. Fifteen right. Turn. Turn. Come on, you stupid lock. I'm standing here in Jockey shorts putting on a show for the entire school. The least you can do is open.*

Spinner arrived and turned his bike into the parking area. "Satch!" he shrieked. "What happened?"

"Gimme your bike and quit asking questions," I ordered.

Staring in disbelief, Spinner handed me the wheels and I jumped on. I pedaled faster than any Olympic champion ever thought of pedaling.

At Water Street, a car stopped and screeched its brakes. The man yelled out his window, "Hey, kid, you'd better slow down and watch where you're going."

I whizzed by. *Sure. Sure. You* try riding across *town in* your *underwear and we'll see how slow and careful you are.*

On Washington Street some kids were jumping up and down inside a station wagon and pointing at me. I could almost hear the little girl shrieking, "Mommy, Mommy, that boy who's been riding across town with the shovel all week is out there today in his underwear."

No, lady this is not the latest craze.

At last I spotted home. I sped into the driveway, threw the bike against the garage, and charged into the house.

"Satch? What are you doing ho—?" Mom stared at my lobster-red legs in astonishment. "What on earth happened?"

"I jumped out of a swing and my jeans didn't."

"Ha. Ha. Ha."

"It's not funny, Mom."

"I'm sorry, honey. It's just so," she tried desperately to conceal her laughter, "so unexpected."

"Mo-om, every girl in the sixth grade has seen me in my underwear!"

"Laugh with them. They'll get over it and that will be the end of it."

"Sure. Sure. The end of it, maybe when I'm thirty."

"Why don't you put on some clean clothes and I'll drive you to school?"

"Mo-om, you don't think I'm going back there, do you?"

"Satch, you'll have to face them sooner or later. You can't hide out at home forever."

"How about just a few years?"

"Satch, get it over with and you won't have to think about it forever."

Hmm . . . I dragged myself upstairs. I *would* have to think about it forever. *Everyone* would have to think about it forever. Motormouth Marcie would see to that. She probably had a cheering section all rehearsed by now to greet my return with: "We haven't seen London, we haven't seen France, but lucky us, we've seen *Siiidney's* underpants."

I peeled off my sweaty T-shirt. Man, was I sticky and hot from that marathon bike race. And I itched all over. I scratched away. I fumbled through my drawer looking for a clean shirt. I scratched some more. How was I gonna face everyone? Maybe even the guys would laugh. Everybody wears underwear. Why was it so embarrassing?

I scratched again. My arms were getting raw. Maybe Mom changed laundry detergents? A long time ago I got hives from a new brand.

"Mo-om?"

"Yes?" she called up the stairs.

"Did you use one of those perfumy soaps again?"

"No."

"Well, did you change fabric softeners?"

"No. What's the matter?"

"I itch all over."

Mom came upstairs. "Let me see." She started inspecting my arms. "*Hmm.* Did you notice this earlier?"

"No."

"Turn around and let me see your back."

"Well?"

"Well." Mom was looking at my stomach now.

"Well? What is it?"

"It's not hives."

"Good."

"It's chicken pox."

"Chicken pox? Only babies get chicken pox."

"Well, Satch, I'm afraid the chicken pox don't know that. You'll have to take a soda bath and stay home a week or so."

"A whole week?"

"More than likely." Mom must have known what I was thinking. "And, Satch, try not to scratch. They'll only get infected."

Man, a whole week before I'd have to face underwear jokes. Maybe Frankie Spinnelli could do something right after all.

12
Captivity

Mom called the school to tell them I had the chicken pox and would they please have Miss Hepburn prepare the lessons for the next week.

I sat in the bathtub most of the morning and slept in the afternoon. I guess I had a fever.

Brring.

Mom answered, "No, Spinner, I don't think he's up to having company. . . . Just a minute, let me ask him."

Mom came into my dark bedroom. "Satch," she whispered, "you awake?"

"Um?" I groaned. Even my vocal cords ached.

"Spinner's on the phone. Do you want to talk?"

"Um."

"Do you remember the combination to your bicycle lock? It's still at school. Spinner will bring it home for you, if you can remember the numbers."

My bike. It had completely slipped my mind. Spinner was a real pal for picking up the pieces I left behind.

"Thirty-two . . . fifteen . . . twenty-nine," I groaned out slowly. "Left first."

"Got it. Start left. Thanks, honey. Now try to go back to sleep."

Sleep. How do you tell a bedtime story to a chicken pox? I kept wishing I had the strength to talk to Spinner. What did the kids say about my sailing through the air in my underwear? Was there anyone who didn't see me? Did they all laugh when they found out I had the chicken pox? Was there any reason in the world I would ever want to return to Roosevelt School? At last, my chicken pox and I drifted into dreamland.

Later that evening I woke to hear Mom on the telephone talking to Dad. I knew she hated to call him, but she couldn't very well make me call, since I was out of it.

"Sid? . . . This is Sara Jane. . . . Satch won't be able to come this weekend. He has the chicken pox. . . . Yes, just this morning. . . . He has a low fever. He's lost his appetite, but I'm managing to keep fluids down him. . . . Well, they're still popping out. He's covered. . . . Maybe Tuesday or Wednesday. . . . OK. 'Bye."

That was the most Mom and Dad had spoken in a

year. Maybe I should get sick more often.

Saturday I felt worse. Everything everywhere itched. When I wasn't sitting in water to relieve the itching, I was drinking water to bring down my fever. I crawled back into bed after Mom coated me with Caladryl lotion. Sleep was about all I could handle.

Sunday I actually looked out my window. Ah, daylight. I was alive after all. Mom came upstairs with some juice.

"Satch, do you think you could eat some scrambled eggs? You haven't had anything in your stomach in two days."

I forced down a gulp of juice. I could feel it passing pox after pox on its way down.

"Yeah, I'll try some eggs," I moaned.

Mom went back downstairs while I scratched. I didn't feel overheated anymore, but I must have had three million more chicken pox pop out since yesterday. And every one of them was screaming, "Me first. Scratch me first."

I dragged myself into the bathroom. I looked in the mirror. Eeek! I was wearing a smashed pizza for a face. Even my freckles had been crowded out. I dabbed more Caladryl lotion on those splotches. My shoulders, my toes, my scalp. It would be a whole lot easier just to buy a case of the stuff and take a bath in it. My eyelids. My earlobes. Yuck, I bet I even had those stupid things under my fingernails.

Mom came upstairs with the eggs. "Here, honey,

try this," she coaxed. She held out a spoonful.

Obediently, I put it into my mouth. I tried to swallow. Ugh! There were chicken pox covering my tongue and lining the roof of my mouth. The food was making its way down my throat as if it were traveling a chicken pox obstacle course. Unfortunately, the food didn't miss any of the obstacles before reaching its destination.

"Mom, I can't." I pushed the eggs away.

"Well, please try to drink your juice. I'm afraid you'll get dehydrated," she fretted.

Hmm . . . dehydrated. Maybe the chicken pox would dry up and fall off. Of course, that meant the rest of me would dry up and fall apart first.

I choked down the juice.

Monday morning, I could hear Carrie and Lisa leaving for school. Ugh, school. I didn't want to think about what I would face when I returned. I slept most all morning. By afternoon I was gaining strength. Another bath and another layer of Caladryl and I could consider becoming human again.

I turned on the Atari. For three days I had left civilization. It was time to return to the great American pastime—video mania.

I pulled out the Asteroids cartridge. "Take that. Bam! Bam! And that. Bam!" Those blobs reminded me too much of chicken pox.

I switched to Congo Bongo. "Tita tita beep. Tita tita beep." The little man wiggled across the screen. He climbed the great coconut barrier and was crossing alligator alley. Oops. Splat. Swallowed up. A chicken pox got him.

No matter what I did, I just couldn't forget those stinking chicken pox. Maybe they were on my brain, too.

Tuesday the chicken pox started to scab over. They still itched, but I thought they were done popping out. That was probably because there was no place left.

I was giving the Atari one more attempt to entertain me when Mom interrupted, "Satch, you have a visitor if you're up to it."

"Really? Who?"

"Spinner."

"Send him in." Finally, communication with the outside world.

Spinner strutted into the family room. "How ya feeling, buddy? Man, you don't look so good."

"In spite of my checkerboard appearance, I am feeling much better."

"Well, if you say so. But you still look a mess."

"Thanks for the vote of confidence." Enough of this chicken pox conversation. I wanted to talk about what was really bugging me. "Hey, Spinner, what did the kids say about me ripping my pants? You know, about me having nothing left but my underwear after I leaped out of the swing?"

"Ha. Ha. It was a pretty hot topic Friday. . . . everybody laughed."

"I thought so."

"Well, Satch, it was rather funny when you think about it," Spinner chuckled.

"Yeah, yeah. It's real funny until it's you." How could my best friend laugh, too?

"Don't worry. No one even mentioned it today."

"Not even Marcie? I thought she'd have it in the newspaper by now."

"She gloated a lot Friday, but she's been really strange the last couple of days. In fact, she wasn't even Marcie. Maybe she was sick or something."

"She might have the chicken pox, too."

"Naw, you can't get 'em twice. She had the chicken pox in the first grade when I did. She's the one who gave 'em to me."

"What did she do that made her so strange?"

"I can't put my finger on it. Marcie was just weird."

"Marcie's always weird."

"I know, but she was a different weird from her usual weird."

"Spinner, you're not making any sense."

"I don't know how to explain it. She just sat there all day in class. She didn't moan. She didn't complain. She didn't wave her hand in the teacher's face. She didn't do anything."

"You mean she didn't even talk?"

"Right. Not to anyone."

"*Hmm* . . . well, if Marcie's not running her motor, we can all be grateful. But I'll have to see it to believe it. This can't last. It's too good to be true."

Spinner and I launched an attack on Asteroids and Congo Bongo.

13
Dinner Is Served

Wednesday morning I awoke to the phone. Mom answered. "Hello? . . . Hi. . . . Better, but he's got a long way to go. . . . Just a minute, I'll see if he's awake."

Mom whispered into my room, "Honey? You awake?"

"Yeah?"

"Dad's on the phone. Would you like him to come over tonight?"

"Yeah."

"OK. I'll tell him."

Man, Mom and Dad were actually talking to each other. Twice even. Of course, they weren't looking at each other. It's easier to be brave when you don't have to look at somebody.

"Sid?" Mom was back to the phone now. "I think he'd enjoy seeing you. . . . OK. . . . Do you want to stay for dinner? Maybe you can coax him into eating."

I would have gone on a hunger strike years ago if I thought it would get Mom and Dad back together. Maybe these chicken pox weren't so bad.

I went into the bathroom to inventory my pox. Only two million left. *Hang on, you little poxies. Only a little while longer until I get Mom and Dad back together.*

I went into Mom's bedroom to find her medical reference book. It was filled with disease after disease, information to describe the problem, and solutions for treatments. *Hmm . . .* if only it told how to catch the stuff. Ah. Here we are. Yellow fever. Good and frightening. Maybe too frightening. Malaria. Now all I needed was a mosquito. But where to find a mosquito in Michigan this time of year? Foiled again. Even if I could find a mosquito, it wouldn't be the right kind.

I gave the pages a flip. Scarlet fever. Sounded simple enough. Fever. Sore throat. Rash. I could scratch my stomach for a rash and eat cherry cough drops for the red throat. How could I engineer a fever? Jumping jacks? I'd have to give it some more thought. But as soon as these chicken pox bit the dust, it would be scarlet fever, here I come.

I read comic books the rest of the afternoon. *Dingdong.*

Dad was here. I ran to the top of the stairs to listen. Mom answered the door.

"Hi, Sid. Come on in."

"Thanks. How's he doing?"

"I think the worst is over, but he'll probably be home from school at least the rest of the week."

Little did they know I would be home at least another month to pull off this little caper. I hopped back in bed, ready to begin my invalid act. Mom and Dad were actually talking face-to-face. Pretty soon, they'd be using whole paragraphs.

"I stopped by school and picked up Satch's assignments."

School? Could he have seen Barb? Naw, he was just there to get my homework. *Hmm* . . . I'd better have Spinner pick up my homework from now on and not take any chances.

"Why don't you head on upstairs? I'll bring you two dinner in a half hour or so."

I could hear the stairs creaking as Dad approached.

"Howdy, fella," Dad greeted me cheerfully. "I hear you have the market cornered on chicken pox."

"Yeah. Look at me. I'm a mess."

"They'll go away, but it'll take some time. You should have seen me when I was a kid."

"Did you look this bad?"

"Oh, a hundred times worse, at least."

Dad put the load of books on my desk. "I had to stop by school anyway, so I picked up your

94

assignments, Satch. Maybe tomorrow, you'll feel like tackling them."

You had to stop by school anyway? All the old fears of Miss Barb Hepburn flooded my mind.

"What were you at school for *anyway*?" I asked.

"Well, I had to talk to your teacher about something."

Something? You mean now he had to go to school to ask her for a date. What was wrong with the telephone? What if the kids saw him?

"What's the 'something'?" I asked bravely.

"Look, Satch, I'd better start at the beginning. We need to talk."

We need to talk. You *need to talk.*

Dad hesitated, "Do you remember I told you I was dating a woman named Barb?"

"Yeah." *How could I forget?*

"I didn't want you to get involved because I was afraid it might cause you difficulty at school. . . ."

You're right there.

"I thought if Barb and I continued to date, summer vacation might be a more appropriate time to tell you."

At least she wouldn't be my teacher anymore.

"But something has happened that makes it necessary to tell you now . . ."

Oh, no. He's gonna get married!

"Before you're in a situation that might be embarrassing for you."

Embarrassing? You mean mortifying.

"The Barb that I'm dating is Barb Cook."

95

Huh? Barb Cook? What does that have to do with school? I don't know any Barb Co— "Do you mean B.J. Cook? Marcie's mother?" I shrieked.

"Yes, Marcie calls her mother B.J."

I fell back against my pillow, like I'd just been pushed off the Empire State Building. This was mind shattering. How could I have been so stupid? Dating my teacher would almost be a relief right now.

"But, Dad—"

"Satch, she's really a very nice person," Dad interrupted.

"But, Marcie is—"

"A very sensitive young lady," he finished my sentence.

"Dad, Marcie is just about the—"

"Most surprised person in the world next to you," Dad finished for me again.

"But, Dad, you don't understand," I protested.

"I do, Satch. It's you who doesn't understand. Just give it time."

Hmm . . . time. That was what they all said. My shoulders dropped five inches. My eyes sank to the floor. All I wanted to do was cry, but it wouldn't help. I'd just look like a baby.

"Well, why did you tell me now? Why didn't you wait till summer? Are you going to get married or something?" Pictures of me being sucked in by the human vacuum cleaner flashed through my mind.

"No, no. Satch. I only told you now because Marcie realized her mother and I were dating. I thought it would be best if you heard it from me, not her. That's all."

Marcie. I could see it all now. She would really have a drama waiting for me when I returned to school. And I thought soaring through the air in my underwear was bad. Little did I know I was flying right into Marcie's clutches.

I could hear her motor humming: "Well, *Siiidney,* now that we're almost related, I suppose you'll expect me to take care of you. I have to admit you do need some looking after. Anyone that is stupid enough to parachute out of a swing without realizing the dangers that await definitely needs a bodyguard. I guess someone has to perform this unwanted chore."

In desperation, I tried one more appeal, "But, Dad, I thought you and Mom were getting along now."

"Satch, your mother and I both realize there's no point in an adversary relationship. We're getting along because we both love you, not because we intend to get remarried."

Silence.

"Satch, I'm sorry it's not what you wanted to hear. I'm sure you'll understand it all in time."

Hmm . . . time. Understand. Here we go again. If I lived to be a hundred, it wouldn't be enough time to understand *this.*

Mom stepped in. "Dinner is served," she announced.

I couldn't eat. It wasn't the chicken pox that

stopped the food from going down anymore. It wasn't even the beginning of scarlet fever. There was a much bigger lump in my throat. I wouldn't have to fake being sick.

14
Outer Space

My pajamas were starting to take on a life of their own, so Thursday I got dressed in real clothes. Everything hung. I guess I had lost weight. I had to tighten my belt two extra notches. I certainly didn't plan on losing my pants ever again.

I sat at my desk and decided to get some of my homework out of the way. Spelling, that was easy. I'd start there. Page 131, Unit 25. Ah. Words beginning with hard G and soft G. Those are a cinch if you know the e-i-y rule from third grade. I read the directions: Number your paper from 1-20. Choose a spelling word for each synonym listed. Write the pair on your paper.

Sounded simple enough. I numbered my paper

and began to pair off synonyms. 1. Naive—GULL-IBLE. . . . Yep, that's me. How could I even think Dad was dating my teacher? 2. Amiable—GRA-CIOUS. . . . Marcie would be waiting to greet me graciously Monday morning. 3. Showy—GAUDY. . . . 4. Apparel—GARMENT. . . . Undoubtedly, she would be wearing her gaudy, red, killer garment. 5. Leader—GOVERNOR. . . . 6. Vagrant—GYPSY. . . . Marcie would govern my life with an iron fist. My only escape was to run away and lead the life of a gypsy.

I put down my pencil. Spelling was exhausting.

I switched to social studies. That would take me worlds away from Marcie. I flipped the page to where we had left off last week, "Desert Regions of the Earth." Soon I was knee deep in sand. The sun was blistering my back. My lips were cracked, my throat parched. Desperately, I cried, "Waaater."

With blurred vision, my rolling eyeballs focused on an outstretched arm. It held a glass of cool, wet, lifesaving water. I reached forward with my last ounce of strength. Just as I felt the tingle of moisture on the tips of my fingers, Marcie drew in her arm, put the glass to her lips, and started gargling.

Ah! She's everywhere. At this rate I would never get my homework done. I would flunk sixth grade. I jumped into bed with my clothes on and pulled the covers over my head. I might as well go to sleep. My "daymares" were worse than my nightmares.

100

Spinner came over Friday after school. The kids had made me get-well cards, and he delivered them.

"Wait till you read this one from Hai. It's a scream," Spinner laughed.

Hai's card had some kid with red blobs all over his face saying, "Never stand at the finish line in a cherry-pit-spitting contest." So that's what he thinks my face looks like, huh.

"And look at A.J.'s," Spinner chuckled. "There's this picture of a masked bandit running from the hospital. He's carrying a hot-water bottle and a thermometer. He's got a blanket thrown over his shoulder. The caption reads, 'Drop your cover and get well soon.'"

Real clever. I knew that A.J. meant, "Drop your drawers again, so we can all have another laugh."

"Satch? You OK?" Spinner asked cautiously.

"I'm OK. Why?"

"You just seem kinda different. I thought these cards would cheer you up. We all miss you a lot."

"Thanks, Spinner. That's nice to know."

I tried to show more enthusiasm for the cards. Maybe I was imagining too much.

I checked over some more cards. Where was Marcie's? I bet she had a few thousand nasty things to say like, "Stay sick if you know what's good for you." I flipped through the papers. There was no card from Marcie. I couldn't have missed it. I fumbled through the papers again. I was right. There was no card from Marcie.

"Spinner, did everyone make a card?"

I didn't want him to think I actually *wanted* a card from Marcie. I just wondered what she'd have to say.

"As far as I know, everyone made one. Well, except for Lizabeth. She went to Detroit today. Her family is looking for a house. They're moving."

"Moving? I didn't know that."

I was sorry to hear about Lizabeth moving. I sort of liked her, I mean like a friend. She wasn't so bad after all.

"Satch? You sure you're OK?"

"Yeah. Why?"

"I don't know. You seem kinda like you're in outer space or something."

I was. I wanted to tell Spinner everything, but I just couldn't come out of orbit.

15
The Invention

I knew Monday would arrive. It always does. But I was hoping the calendar would flip right into July when February ended. That way I wouldn't have to return to school. Unfortunately, March appeared the way it does every year. I was going to have to face Marcie, like it or not.

I left home five minutes before the opening bell. I didn't want even one extra minute on that playground.

Brrring.

I rounded the corner to the bike racks. Most of the kids were already filing in the door.

"Satch," Spinner called through the crowd. He waited at the entryway. "I was worried you weren't

103

gonna show up. I thought maybe you had to stay home another day."

Don't I wish.

We walked down the hallway.

Spinner started talking about softball teams. I couldn't concentrate on anything he was saying.

My mind was on one thing—facing Marcie. What was gonna happen? As soon as I entered that room, it would be all over. Marcie would fry me in the electric chair. I held my breath and stepped forward, resigned to meeting my fate.

Hmm . . . Marcie didn't notice me. She was too busy twirling her hair around her pencil. I walked on padded feet to my desk. I slipped into my seat. She had to know I was here by now. My back was only inches away from her face. If I stayed turned around, I'd be safe. What was I thinking? Marcie would use her dandruff-coated pencil to poke holes in my back. In five minutes I'd be a human pincushion.

Miss Hepburn started class. "Let's open our spelling books to Unit 26, please."

Desks rumbled. Pages flew. But no pencil in the back. Marcie was probably arranging her weaponry: chewed bubble gum to stick me to my chair, a feather to tickle my ear, and tweezers to pluck my hair out one strand at a time.

Spelling class ticked away. No gum. No feather. No tweezers. She must be back there designing a new means of torture.

English class began. *Hmm* . . . No foghorn

104

blaring in my ear. No feet banging on my chair. No paper clips hanging from my ears. Whatever Marcie was planning back there, it must be a doozie, sure to create real agony for Satch Carlton.

Miss Hepburn went on to math. Still no heavy breathing. No spiders leaping over my shoulder. No multiplication problems solved on my shirt.

Where was Marcie? Maybe she wasn't there anymore. Maybe she slipped out and I didn't notice. I wanted to turn around and check. But if I turned around and she *was* there, I'd have to look at her face-to-face. Ugh! That was too risky.

I put my head down low to my desk. I looked like I was really into my assignment. I tried to peer underneath my arm. All I could see was the upper corner of her desk. Gotta have a better look. I stretched and tried to put my head into my armpit. I could see no more, and I was gonna end up a pretzel.

Aha. Why didn't I think of it before? The old drop-the-pencil-on-the-floor-accidentally trick.

Plunk. Over the edge it went. I started stretching to get myself in spying position.

"Your pencil, Satch?" Hai asked. He bent down and retrieved it.

"Thanks," I mumbled. So much for that trick.

I glared into the glass showcase two aisles over. Maybe I could see Marcie's reflection? Naw. The light was all wrong. A mirror. That's what I needed. But where would I get a mirror? Lizabeth. Girls always have that stuff in their purses.

I dashed off a note: Lizabeth, can I borrow your mirror? It's a matter of life and death. Satch.

I couldn't get caught this time. Gradually, I slipped the note forward in my row. "Pass it to Lizabeth," I whispered through my teeth.

I watched the note reach Lizabeth. She read it and gave me an are-you-crazy? look. But she sent the mirror. Good old Lizabeth. I'd miss her when she moved.

"Class," Miss Hepburn announced, "we have one more item to cover before we break for recess."

The mirror reached my desk.

"We are beginning a new unit in science on inventors and their inventions. . . ."

I opened the plastic clasp on the mirror. It was part of a woman's makeup case. Yuck! I didn't want to look like I was putting on powder or something, but I was desperate. I had to use it anyway.

"I'm sure you're familiar with the very famous inventors like Henry Ford, Thomas Edison, and the Wright Brothers, but I'd like you to do some research on some lesser-known inventors. . . ."

I cupped the mirror in my left hand, as I nervously chewed on my right.

"Their inventions account for many of the modern conveniences we take for granted, like the furnace, or the toaster. . . ."

I rested my forehead on the side of my wrist while peering into the mirror concealed in my hand.

Miss Hepburn continued, " . . . Some inventions

106

we have become so accustomed to that we rarely stop and realize someone had to think up the idea, like the safety pin, the needle and thread, the zipper. . . ."

I couldn't see a thing. It was a total blur. The mirror was too close. I bit my nail while I considered a new approach.

". . . The interesting thing to note, however, is the determination shown by the individual to succeed no matter what hardships or degradations he might encounter along the way. . . ."

I stretched out my hand in front of me. My face was reflecting back at me. All I had to do was lean to the side, and I'd have a clear shot of Marcie.

". . . In some instances, the inventors were ridiculed, and the inventions were viewed as totally impractical. But because the inventor persevered, we have some very remarkable things. . . ."

I swiveled to my left. Aha. Marcie *was* behind me. She was sitting there doing *absolutely nothing*.

". . . In fact we are most fortunate to have in our midst our very own determined young inventor, Satch Carlton. . . ."

Huh?

"Do you suppose you could reveal the identity of your latest triumph? By chance, do you have in your hand the answer to detecting premature balding?"

The class roared.

"Or could you have invented the secret formula to keep that young and lovely skintone of youth?"

The class howled again.

"Maybe it's the newest CIA extrasensory-eyes-in-the-back-of-my-head device?"

She had me there.

"Well, since you don't seem to have it quite perfected yet, I suggest you keep it under wraps so that no one beats you to the patent office. Right?"

I nodded understanding. Miss Hepburn—what style. Any other teacher would just grab the mirror and toss it in the basket. But not her. She knew how to turn a simple mirror into a you'd-better-pay-attention-or-else machine.

16
The Meeting of Minds

Miss Hepburn dismissed the class for recess. I stood up to casually glance back at Marcie. She just stared straight ahead. *Hmm . . .* she wasn't even getting ready to go. Slowly, I headed for the door. Marcie still wasn't moving. She sat there like a zombie.

"What's happened to Marcie?" I nudged Spinner.

"I warned you, Satch," Spinner reminded me. "Marcie's been acting really weird."

"Yeah, but I never expected *this.*"

"Well, something strange is going on. Her brain has been hypnotized for more than a week."

Could it be Marcie was thinking about her mom

and dad, too? It was just about a week since I found out. I could think about nothing else. But at least if we had an earthquake, I'd know it. The whole world could crumble away, and Marcie would still be locked in her trance.

The rest of the day was the same story. Marcie sitting motionless and everyone else wondering why. I didn't like knowing. It was spooky, even eerie. I always thought being a mind reader would be neat. It wasn't. Somehow, I felt guilty for Marcie sitting there like that. I almost wanted her to stick her tongue out at me or tape a KICK ME PLEASE! sign on my back. Then I'd know she was back to normal, and I wasn't responsible for her flipping out.

Tuesday was a rerun of Monday. I kept turning around nonchalantly to check on the blob. No sign of life. She just stared and said nothing. Man, she was really gone. I had been in outer space for a while, but Marcie was out of the universe.

Just before dismissal, Miss Hepburn asked me, "Satch, could you stay after class a moment? I, ah, need to discuss your, ah, makeup assignments from last week."

Hmm . . . I turned them all in yesterday. And I even used my best penmanship. I wondered what was wrong.

I sauntered up to Miss Hepburn's desk after school.

"Satch, thank you for staying," Miss Hepburn began.

"Is something wrong?"

"Yes," Miss Hepburn sighed. "But it's not about your homework. I need to talk with you about something else, and I didn't want the rest of the class to wonder what this discussion was all about."

"Oh." This sounded serious.

Miss Hepburn drew in a deep breath and started again. "Satch, I have a problem, and I'm hoping you can help me."

"Me?"

"Your dad stopped by last week to explain that he and Marcie's mother were dating."

"Yeah?"

"He thought I should know, in case the two of you needed time to adjust. You appear to be handling the situation well, but I'm very worried about Marcie. She is dangerously withdrawing into herself."

I nodded agreement.

"This is a very critical time for her. I wondered if you had any ideas? She needs help coping with this change. You're a natural-born leader, Satch— smart, creative, magnetic. Everyone likes you, even me, no matter what you do." She twinkled a knowing smile at me. "But, poor Marcie, no matter how hard she tries, people reject her."

Yeah. Miss Hepburn was right. No one except Lizabeth could stand to be around Marcie. I was always so busy trying to avoid her, that I never realized she acted that way to try to *make* friends. Instead she was driving people away.

"And now Marcie has stopped trying altogether. She thinks her world is falling apart. First her father deserts her. Then Lizabeth announces she's moving. And now, she sees the one person left in her life who accepts her being taken away by some man. I realize that's a bit of an exaggeration, Satch, but in Marcie's eyes, that's what's happening."

Hmm . . . I never really tried to think about Marcie's feelings. I was always too busy concentrating on some clever remark to fling back at her. I guess she was pretty miserable.

Miss Hepburn sighed, "I'm really worried about her, Satch."

"Don't worry. I'll think on it," I answered.

"Thanks, Satch. I knew I could count on you."

As I rode down Oliver Street, pictures of Marcie in her suspended-animation state flashed through my mind. She really did look terrible. And I always thought I *wanted* her motor turned off.

The warm breeze swished through my hair. Spring was just around the corner. March 4th already. March 4th? Man alive! The rummage sale was in two more days. I had to get cracking. I pedaled with renewed vigor toward the church.

"Hi, Reverend Miller," I puffed out.

"Satch," his face brightened, "glad to see you on your feet. I heard you had quite a bad case of chicken pox."

"You heard right."

"We've missed you the last couple Sundays. I have no idea how to organize a rummage sale."

112

"That's why I stopped. I mean, the rummage sale is why I stopped."

"Good," Reverend Miller smiled.

"Do you know anything about the posters?" I asked.

"I think Marcie Cook passed them out a week ago Sunday. Each person took one poster to an assigned store. She's a dandy little organizer, too."

"Yeah, I know." Maybe Marcie could do something right after all.

"The Redeemer kids weren't here last Sunday, though, so I'm not sure about definite work schedules. Let me see." He started fumbling through a pile of papers. "Ah, here they are. The sign-up sheets you sent around." He handed them to me.

"Thanks."

I looked down at the list. A lot of empty spaces. I would have to do some mighty fancy talking to convince kids they wanted to work extra shifts.

"I'll make some phone calls to remind the kids," I said. "See ya Wednesday night."

"Alrighty, Satch."

I dashed out the door and headed for home again. Reverend Miller was some kinda guy. He had a way of making people have confidence in themselves. My mind played back the time he was patting me on the shoulder, saying he was proud of me for caring about the Lings. He said, *Lots of people talk about loving their fellow man, but it's not always easy to live up to that principle in our daily lives.*

Man, don't I know it. Here I was trying to help Hai's family on the other side of the world, and every day of my life I had never realized *Marcie needed help just as badly.* I was glad to be raising money for the Lings because money could solve some of their problems. *But, God, what does Marcie need? She needs a friend, a real friend who accepts her the way she is.* Somehow, the Lings' problems seemed easily solved. Marcie's didn't.

I ran in the house and grabbed the phone. "Spinner?"

"Oh, hi, Satch," Spinner answered.

"Did you forget about the rummage sale?"

"Yeow! Is that this week?"

"It sure is, and there's a lot to do."

"What do ya need?"

"Would you call the kids from Redeemer?"

"Sure. What do ya want me to tell them?"

I gave Spinner a list of work schedules and directions for dropping off the rummage on Wednesday after school.

"Well, I'll hang up and get right on this," Spinner said.

"Thanks, Spinner, I knew I could count on you. Check with you tomorrow at school. OK?"

"OK."

"Oh, one more thing, Spinner. You don't have to call Marcie. *I'll* call her."

"What did you say?"

"I said I'll call Marcie myself."

"You must be crazy, but be my guest."

114

17
Nothing to Lose, Everything to Gain

I phoned the kids from my church reminding them about the rummage sale. Most of them remembered, but some still hadn't even started cleaning out closets.

I saved Marcie's call for last. *Hmm . . .* where to begin? Just call and get it over with.

"Hello?"

"Mrs. Cook? I mean, B.J.?"

"Yes?"

"This is Satch Carlton."

"Hi, Satch. It's nice to talk with you."

"Is Marcie there, please?"

"Yes, I'll go get her. Just a moment."

I could hear the phone laid down and footsteps

walking away. In another minute, the footsteps returned.

"Hello?"

"Marcie?"

"Yes."

"This is Satch."

Silence.

"Marcie, I called to remind you about the rummage sale."

Silence.

"Can you get your things to the church Wednesday?"

"I don't know."

"Do you need some help?"

"NO!" she shouted.

"If you'd like me to carry something I could probably get my sister to drive over—"

"I don't need your help," she interrupted.

"I wonder if you could work at the sale Thursday morning? That'll be the busiest time, and we don't have too many people signed up."

"I don't know."

"We could really use your help."

Silence again.

"Look, Marcie, I really *need* you."

"Well, I'll have to think about it."

She hung up.

Wednesday morning Marcie walked in the classroom. Her eyes were still glued to the floor. She sank into her seat without a word.

Bravely, I turned around, "Ah, Marcie, can you

come over to the church tonight?"

"Um-m-m, I don't know," her voice mumbled as her head hung down.

"I'm really worried about this rummage sale. I mean, what if it flops? I don't know anything about prices or how many kids we need or if we'll have enough stuff or if we'll have too much stuff."

Maybe I was pouring it on too thick. Marcie just sat there ignoring me. Miss Hepburn smiled at me and started class. I turned back around.

Spinner came up to me at recess.

"Satch, what on earth is going on between you and Marcie? Last night the phone call, and now you're actually turning around and talking to her?"

"It's not what you think."

"Then what is it?"

"Look, Spinner, you know how weird Marcie's been acting lately?"

"Of course I know how weird Marcie's been acting lately; I'm the one who told you."

"Well, I know why."

"You do? Out with it. What's happened to make Marcie flip out?"

"I can't tell you, Spinner. At least, not now."

"You can't tell me? But I'm your best friend."

"And that's why you'll have to trust me. Marcie has to deal with this problem first."

"Then how come you know?"

"I just do. That's all I can tell you now."

"Satch, you're not making any sense."

"Maybe not, but the fact still remains; Marcie

117

needs to know she has some friends."

"Well, let somebody else be her friend."

"That's just it, Spinner. There is nobody else. Lizabeth's the only person in the room who even talks to Marcie, and now Lizabeth's moving."

"But there's nothing about Marcie to like. She's one hundred percent obnoxious."

"I know it's gonna be hard, Spinner, but maybe she's only ninety-nine percent obnoxious. We have to at least try to find that lowly one percent. There must be something about her that's good. Look at it this way—we've got nothing to lose and everything to gain. We can't ask for better odds."

"OK. OK." Spinner relented. "I'll give it a go, if it's that important to you. This is certainly mystifying."

Spinner and I hurried to the church right after school. Dad dropped off my junk just as we were getting out the banquet tables.

"How goes it, kiddo?"

"Well, we're just setting things up," I answered.

While we were talking, five more parents dropped their rummage off.

"Satch, you sure you have enough help?"

"To tell you the truth, Dad, I'm not sure about anything."

"Look, I have to finish this project at work. I'll try to get back here later tonight and see how you're doing. OK?"

"Great. Thanks, Dad."

He hurried off.

118

Seven more families delivered their contributions.

"Hey, Spinner, where are we gonna put this stuff. We're running out of room."

"How about the kitchen?"

"Guess we'll have to."

So the rummage started growing in the kitchen. At five o'clock, the church secretary came downstairs. "Satch?" she asked.

"Yes?"

"Reverend Miller called from the hospital. He's been detained. He said he won't be here until tomorrow. I've locked all the doors. The west door is standing open. You can close it when people are done unloading. It will lock automatically from the outside, but you can still open it from the inside. OK?"

"OK."

The secretary left. More and more things arrived. Even the nursery school rooms were filled. People came, unloaded their vehicles, and left. No one stayed but Spinner and me.

Mom drove up in the station wagon around six o'clock. "Satch, I brought some food for you and Spinner."

"Burgers and fries. Terrific! But, Mom, where's the sundae?"

Mom flashed me her you're-lucky-you-got-this-much-junk-food look. She explained, "I promised Carrie and Lisa I'd drive part of the team to the swim meet. When do you think you'll be done?"

"Late, Mom. There's tons of stuff. We're just about buried alive in there." Panic was starting to churn inside of me.

"Oh, Satch, I'm sorry. I'll come as soon as we get back. Can you get a ride home with Spinner if I'm not around when you're done?"

"Yeah, sure," I sighed.

"Good luck, honey." Mom drove off. Spinner and I chowed down the burgers and fries. The deliveries were starting to slow down. One last person peered over the crates of wrinkled clothes, truckloads of broken-down furniture, and mountains of mismatched shoes.

"Land sakes alive!" Mrs. Cook shrieked. "You certainly have a terrific turnout of things to sell. You'll be able to buy the airplane to bring the Lings to Michigan. When is your pricing and sorting committee coming?"

"Pricing and sorting committee?" I looked at Spinner helplessly. He looked back just as pathetically. "The kids are all scheduled for Thursday, Friday, and Saturday."

"You mean you two fellas are going to organize and display all this rummage *by yourselves?*" Mrs. Cook's eyeballs about fell out.

"It looks that way." I sighed.

"Satch, would you like some help? I think you're going to need it," she hinted.

"Would you? I mean, that would be super. I had no idea this would be so—so—so monstrous."

"I'd be happy to help. Let me buzz home and get

120

Marcie. Mandy can stay next door with the neighbors."

"Ah, Mrs. Cook. I mean, B.J.?"

"Yes?"

"Would you mind if I called Marcie and asked her myself? I just want her to know Spinner and I really *want* her to come. OK?"

"That's very thoughtful of you, Satch. She hasn't been herself lately." B.J. smiled. "You know, Satch, I think your dad was right."

"Huh?"

"He said you were a terrific kid. Now I know why."

"Thanks." I was a little embarrassed. Maybe Dad was right about B.J., too. She was pretty nice about offering to help.

I went to the phone to make one more plea. Nothing to lose and everything to gain. "Marcie?"

Silence.

"This is Satch."

"So?"

"Spinner and I are down here at the rummage sale. We're up to our earlobes in junk. I mean it. The place looks like Miami Beach after a tidal wave. Marcie, I'm not kidding. We really need you."

"I'll think about it."

She hung up.

18
Teamwork

Spinner decided to make a frantic plea to his parents. "Mom, the sale starts tomorrow morning, and we won't be done until Christmas."

It worked. His parents packed up and were at the church in fifteen minutes. Frankie started riding a broken tricycle immediately, but at least we had two more workers.

"Spinner," Mrs. Spinnelli exclaimed, "you said you needed help, but by the looks of things, you need an army."

"*Aaaah!*"

I turned suddenly to see Marcie gasping in surprise. She had come after all.

"B.J.," Mrs. Spinnelli sighed, "am I glad to see

you. Can you believe all this?"

"We really have our work cut out for us, don't we?" B.J. answered.

"I don't know about you, but I'll never make it without a cup of coffee," Mrs. Spinnelli shook her head.

She and B.J. headed for the kitchen. "Ah, there's more," I heard from behind the swinging door.

"I think I'd better go upstairs and close that door," Mr. Spinnelli announced. "There can't be any rummage left in this town. There must be twenty houses sitting absolutely vacant." He dashed up the stairs.

"Well, Marcie," I tried to break the ice, "what d'ya think?"

"I think we'll be here thirty years."

"What should we do?"

"Surrender," Marcie moaned.

"Seriously, where do we begin?"

"Well, the first thing to do is plan where you want things," Marcie stated flatly.

"But how?"

Marcie's ideas came pouring out. "First, sort the clothing into men's, women's, girls', and boys'. Have a long table for each. Then you can divide the sections into summer and winter and tops and bottoms. Oh, you'll also need a table for baby things. That sells really good, so put the baby things on the far side of the room. That way people have to walk by a whole *lot* more stuff before they get to the real reason they came. Who knows,

123

someone might find an item they didn't even know existed."

"That's great," Spinner cheered.

"What else should we do?" I kept asking.

"You'll need an area for toys, an area for furniture, and some more long tables for miscellaneous things—dishes and tools and junk like that."

"Wow. You really know how to run a sale."

The adults came out of the kitchen carrying coffee cups. "Put me to work," ordered Mr. Spinnelli. "Tell me what to do, and we'll get cracking."

I explained Marcie's plan, and we all dug in. What a team. The women sized and sorted clothing while the guys moved furniture. Frankie even sorted out Lego blocks from the puzzle pieces. When we were done with that, Spinner and I unpacked dishes and hung up coats on the clothing racks. Marcie arranged jewelry, and Mr. Spinnelli set up a baby crib.

By ten o'clock we were just short of victory. The team was near total collapse, but the end was in sight. Mr. Spinnelli let out a giant yawn. "Hey, Spinner, let's you and me run out and get a pizza. We'll be back in time to celebrate. What do ya say, team?"

"Yeah!" rang out loud and clear.

"Me go. Me go," whined Frankie.

"No, Frankie, you stay here and help Satch." Mr. Spinnelli winked at me.

"Frankie, I need your help. I can't find the wheel to this car. Can you find it, Frankie?" I pleaded.

Frankie looked dissatisfied but stepped away to search for the missing part.

Spinner and Mr. Spinnelli slipped out for the pizza parlor. The moms strolled into the kitchen to brew another pot of coffee.

"Come on, Marcie, let's mate those shoes over there," I suggested, "and we'll be done."

Marcie still wasn't convinced she wanted to talk to me, but she followed anyway. I picked up a three-inch spiked heel. "How do women walk in these things?"

"Very carefully."

"And look at this orange monstrosity. I can't believe some foot actually wore this."

Marcie chuckled.

"Satch?" Frankie came up to me. "What's this?"

"I don't know. It looks like a bean."

"Bean. A magic bean?"

"Yep, Frankie. It's a magic bean, like *Jack and the Beanstalk*. Plant it in the ground tomorrow and watch it grow to the sky."

"No magic bean like that," Frankie pouted.

"Oh?" That used to be Frankie's favorite story.

"No. Magic bean disappear," Frankie announced. "Watch me. Frankie makes magic." He waved his hands and spun around. "Abrakadabra! Gone. Magic."

"Wow, Frankie. That was great. Where's the bean?"

"Gone. Magic."

"I know, Frankie, but where'd it go?"

125

"Frankie's magic."

"Come on, tell Satch."

"No, Frankie's secret."

"Please?" I begged.

"Guess."

"OK. Your pocket?"

"Nope."

"Your T-shirt?"

"Nope."

"Then where?"

"My nose."

"Your nose?"

"Like magic. Right up there." He even pointed.

"You can't put a bean up your nose!"

"Can so."

I turned to Marcie. "We've got to get that bean out of there. It could be dangerous."

Marcie coaxed, "Frankie, honey, you've got to blow your nose."

He tried. No bean.

"Pretend you're sneezing, Frankie," I pleaded.

Aaachoo. No bean.

"Shake your head." I demonstrated.

He shook. No bean.

"Shake your head and kick one foot." I demonstrated again. "You know, Frankie, like you have water in your ear."

"But I don't have water in ear. I have bean in nose."

"Let's tip him upside down and jolt it out of him," I suggested.

"I don't think that'll work," Marcie said.

"We're gonna have to poke something up there."

"Not my finger." Marcie backed away.

"Frankie, are you sure you really put the bean up your nose?" I was getting a little suspicious.

"Frankie makes magic. Frankie no lie."

I leaned under his nose and peered into his nostrils. Yuck! "I don't see any bean. I don't think it's in there."

"FRANKIE DOESN'T LIE. FRANKIE MAKES GOOD MAGIC." He started to cry.

"Come on, Frankie, where's the bean?"

Frankie was so mad he stomped his feet in a tantrum and screamed at the top of his lungs, "FRANKIE DOESN'T LIE. FRANKIE MAKES GOOD MAG—"

Out popped the bean.

"*Satch, you did it,*" screeched Marcie.

She actually called me *Satch*.

Mrs. Spinnelli came running out of the kitchen. "What happened?"

"Frankie had a bean up his nose," Marcie explained.

"A bean? Oh, my poor baby." She bent down to comfort him. "How in the world did a bean ever get up your nose, honey?"

"Magic. See?" Frankie stuffed the bean back in.

Oh, no. Marcie and I looked at each other. Here we go again.

Bang. Bang. I ran to open the door while Marcie assisted Mrs. Spinnelli in the bean removal.

There was Spinner juggling two giant boxes in his arms. "Quick. Grab this one," Spinner ordered. "It's gonna drop on the floor."

I rescued Spinner. *Clank.* The door closed. Spinner and I looked at each other and laughed. We were locked out. *Bang. Bang.* We pounded for someone else to come.

Dad and Mr. Spinnelli were soon out of their cars and with us at the door. "Dad, you made it," I smiled.

"Yeah. I ran into Spinner and his dad at the pizza parlor. We had the same idea."

"Good stomachs think alike," I joked.

Bang. Bang. Spinner tried again to get the attention of someone inside. We saw someone come up the steps.

"What are you doing out there?" Marcie called through the door.

"Trying to get back in," I smirked.

Marcie laughed, "All right, Houdini, we've had enough magic for one night." She held the door for us to enter.

Spinner and I spread out the paper plates and napkins. We all dove into the pepperoni and cheese.

Mrs. Spinnelli started to tell Frankie's bean-in-the-nose story.

"How in the world did he get—"

"DON'T ASK!" Marcie and I hollered out in unison.

"Get the bean first," I suggested.

So Frankie provided the explanation without the bean. We all applauded the performance.

"Well, kids, you all prepared for tomorrow's big sale?" Dad asked.

"I hope so," Spinner sighed.

"We'd better be," Marcie added.

"Except for one thing," I spoke up.

Worried looks spread across the room.

"We need a cashier. Marcie, you've got to take charge of the money. You're the only one who'll be able to keep it straight."

Spinner glanced over at me. His eyes flickered understanding. "Come on, Marcie. You don't think that two guys who lock themselves out of a building could keep track of real money, do you?"

"OK. OK," Marcie smiled.

"Great!"

We headed out to the parking lot. Mom was just driving up as we let the church door lock.

"Hi, folks," she yelled out the window. "I see I'm here just in time."

"Don't worry, we'll save you some work on the cleanup detail," Mrs. Spinnelli kidded.

Dad walked me over to Mom's car.

"Who won the swim meet?" he asked.

"Not Owosso. But Lisa took second in the freestyle, and Carrie beat her best time in the 'fly."

"Super. Congratulate them for me."

Dad shut the car door for me.

" 'Bye. See ya later." We waved and drove out of the parking lot.

129

"Satch, I really feel badly that I couldn't help tonight. Do you need a hand tomorrow?"

"That'd be great, Mom. But you know what I really need right now?"

"What's that?"

"A hot-fudge sundae. I'm still starved."

Mom tousled my hair and headed the car downtown.

130

SATCH AND THE NEW KID

A new kid in town . . .

And he's the same age as Satch, Spinner, Pete, and A.J.—the Fearless Foursome. He'll fit right in—spitting cherry pits for distance, joining the secret club, and avoiding pests of little brothers. Best of all, he's a soccer star—just what the team needs to win this year's championship.

But something's wrong between the new kid and A.J., and Satch feels caught in the middle. He likes Hai—the new kid. But he likes A.J., too, and he's known A.J. forever. Can't he be friends with both of them? Why can't they get along?

It looks like trouble coming—fast!

Read about Satch and the gang
in these exciting books!

Satch and the New Kid
Satch and the Motormouth

KAREN SOMMER teaches third graders and has twin boys of her own. Her writing career began when her students begged for more of the stories she composed for class. She's been writing ever since!